FATHER'S DREAM

SEAL Brotherhood: Legacy Series
Book 8

SHARON HAMILTON

SHARON HAMILTON'S BOOK LIST

SEAL BROTHERHOOD BOOKS

SEAL BROTHERHOOD SERIES
Accidental SEAL Book 1
Fallen SEAL Legacy Book 2
SEAL Under Covers Book 3
SEAL The Deal Book 4
Cruisin' For A SEAL Book 5
SEAL My Destiny Book 6
SEAL of My Heart Book 7
Fredo's Dream Book 8
SEAL My Love Book 9
SEAL Encounter Prequel to Book 1
SEAL Endeavor Prequel to Book 2
Ultimate SEAL Collection Vol. 1 Books 1-4 /2 Prequels
Ultimate SEAL Collection Vol. 2 Books 5-9

SEAL BROTHERHOOD LEGACY SERIES
Watery Grave Book 1
Honor The Fallen Book 2
Grave Injustice Book 3
Deal With The Devil Book 4
Cruisin' For Love Book 5
Destiny of Love Book 6
Heart of Gold Book 7
Father's Dream Book 8

BAD BOYS OF SEAL TEAM 3 SERIES
SEAL's Promise Book 1

SEAL My Home Book 2

SEAL's Code Book 3

Big Bad Boys Bundle Books 1-3

BAND OF BACHELORS SERIES
Lucas Book 1

Alex Book 2

Jake Book 3

Jake 2 Book 4

Big Band of Bachelors Bundle

BONE FROG BROTHERHOOD SERIES
New Year's SEAL Dream Book 1

SEALed At The Altar Book 2

SEALed Forever Book 3

SEAL's Rescue Book 4

SEALed Protection Book 5

Bone Frog Brotherhood Superbundle

BONE FROG BACHELOR SERIES
Bone Frog Bachelor Book 0.5

Unleashed Book 1

Restored Book 2

Revenge Book 3

Legacy Book 4

NOVELLAS
SEAL You In My Dreams Magnolias and Moonshine

PARANORMALS

FREE TO LOVE SERIES
Free As A Bird Book 1
Romance Book 2
Science Of The Heart Book 3
The Promise Directive Book 4
New Beginnings Book 5

GOLDEN VAMPIRES OF TUSCANY SERIES
Honeymoon Bite Book 1
Mortal Bite Book 2
Christmas Bite Book 3
Midnight Bite Book 4

THE GUARDIANS
Heavenly Lover Book 1
Underworld Lover Book 2
Underworld Queen Book 3
Redemption Book 4

FALL FROM GRACE SERIES
Gideon: Heavenly Fall

SUNSET BEACH SERIES
I'll Always Love You

Back To You

NOVELLAS
SEAL Of Time Trident Legacy

All of Sharon's books are available on Audible,
narrated by the talented J.D. Hart.

ABOUT THE BOOK

Navy SEAL Fredo Chavez and his wife, Mia, learn how far their love will stretch to include an unloved orphan, abandoned and abused. They open their hearts to this little one, only to find the whole world bloom in unexpected ways.

Balancing work and being a family, Fredo must make the difficult distinction which is more important. He considers the heartbreaking decision of retirement, detaching from his brotherhood of warriors, until this little addition teaches him the value of being a true blue dad in all ways possible.

Once again, love comes to this elite operator's rescue.

AUTHOR'S NOTE

I always dedicate my SEAL Brotherhood books to the brave men and women who defend our shores and keep us safe. Without their sacrifice and that of their families—because a warrior's fight always includes his or her family—I wouldn't have the freedom and opportunity to make a living writing these stories. They sometimes pay the ultimate price so we can debate, argue, go have coffee with friends, raise our children, and see them have children of their own.

One of my favorite tributes to warriors resides on many memorials, including one I saw honoring the fallen of WWII on an island in the Pacific:

> "When you go home
> Tell them of us, and say,
> For your tomorrow,
> We gave our today."

These are my stories created out of my own imagination. Anything that is inaccurately portrayed is either my mistake or done intentionally to disguise something I might have overheard over a beer or in the corner of one of the hangouts along the Coronado Strand.

I support two main charities. Navy SEAL/UDT Museum operates in Ft. Pierce, Florida. Please learn about this wonderful museum, all run by active and former SEALs and their friends and families, and who rely on public support, not that of the U.S. Government. www.navysealmuseum.org

IF YOU GOT ANY CLOSER, YOU WOULD HAVE TO ENLIST

I also support Wounded Warriors, who tirelessly bring together the warrior as well as the family members who are just learning to deal with their soldier's condition and have nowhere to turn. It is a long path to becoming well, but I've seen first-hand what this organization does for its warriors and the families who love them. Please give what your heart tells you is right. If you cannot give, volunteer at one of the many service centers all over the United States. Get involved. Do something meaningful for someone who gave so much of themselves, to families who have paid the price for your freedom. You'll find a family there unlike any other on the planet. www.woundedwarriorproject.org

CHAPTER 1

FREDO CHAVEZ AND the rest of his unit on SEAL Team 3 waited in the bushes for nightfall. Reportedly, the cartel boss, Alejandro Ochoa, was a former cop who was caught embezzling US funds designed to put the cartels out of business and who served several years in prison for his crime then was pardoned by the Mexican president as a favor to the local governor. He took up his new job as representative of the cartel, helping migrants make the trek to the US by being their sponsor, collecting fees, and arranging the coyotes to deliver them to the Rio Grande for a border crossing.

It was also said he always showed up at dusk the night before the travel and they often started their trek at night. He was known for wearing bright green alligator boots.

As the team waited, Fredo readied his camera. The light began to dim in the sky, bringing with it some coolness, which was welcome. His job was to take pictures of the cartel boss, send them to the head shed, get confirmation a transfer of cash or other collateral occurred, and then have the team move against Ochoa as soon as he left the band of migrants.

The forty or so migrants in this particular group were mostly young men, women, and children, some appearing as young as two years old.

Fredo inhaled deeply and bit his lip as he watched through the telephoto lens. The terrified faces of the young children haunted him, their eyes wide. Hushed, afraid to make a noise, they hovered close to their mothers, those that had them. Others who were strays were quickly adopted into a family unit, rarely with a male member. He could see there was a great deal of distrust among the migrant children for any of the males, even the trafficked males in this group.

Some crying caught Fredo's attention, and he moved the camera so he could see the young child, a girl, crying next to her presumed older brother, who was about ten. The kid was searching all around him while he held her hand, trying to convince her to stop crying, but she was clearly upset about something. It didn't take long before they all realized what was causing the children so much anxiety.

Through the bushes came a bloodied female, someone who'd been obviously beaten, pushed, and prodded by being kicked in her rear end nearly to the point of making her fall by two coyote guards, who laughed at her stumbling. All of a sudden, a cry went out, and the entire group was yelled at and asked to form a line. The woman was sobbing. Bloody tears ran down her cheeks, leaving red stains on her white shirt. She collapsed and fell at the feet of her children.

Fredo's heart lurched, and he felt his stomach drop to his ankles.

"Fucking assholes. These people are animals."

He knew this woman would pay dearly for her passage, and that didn't include the horrific cost of rape that had probably just occurred. It may not have been the first time, either, as several of the other women looked like they were sporting bruises to their eyes and arms, and a couple of them were limping. There was general suffering all around. Their State Department liaison had warned them the condition of the migrants could tear their heart out.

They were right, Fredo thought.

No one in the group looked at each other, the most common trajectory was either to their own family members or the ground. And everyone tried to stay as quiet as they could as they formed their bloodied, sad, ragtag line.

The woman with the two children could not stop her sobbing, but she managed to do it in silence, holding both of them close to her thighs as she stood tall, wiping the tears from her face and the blood from her nose with part of her apron she wore over her skirt. She had no shoes, Fredo recognized, and that was going to be a problem. There was no way she was going to be able to trek across the desert-like area populated with cactus, broken shards of rock, and animal carcasses that would be their trajectory until they got to the Rio Grande valley crossing, where it would begin to soften and green up slightly. Her feet would long be in shreds before then.

Fredo looked at the two men who had escorted her from the bushes, and they were talking to themselves, sharing something, and he wondered what they were looking at. They appeared to be examining papers. Had they had possibly stripped them from the woman? Fredo didn't know, and he could not hear their words. Once in a while, he could catch some of the louder conversation. He wished he had a voice accelerator to hear everything, but for this mission, they were traveling very light, and it wasn't required.

Now he wished he'd insisted. He could get better intel that way.

The lead gunman, one of six guards who were traveling with the group, with an AK-47 strapped across his midsection, shouted for their attention.

The whole team heard a vehicle approach. It

sounded like a Humvee, and they recognized it as the sound of freedom in their battles in Iraq, Afghanistan, and Africa.

But instead of being the sound and sight of freedom, it was a black Humvee customized with extra chrome and huge wheels, lifted, and Fredo was sure it had been stolen from US forces somewhere or driven across the border as a stolen vehicle. This had to be Alejandro Ochoa.

The whole team had been made aware Ochoa liked to collect the fees himself, oftentimes accepting extra monies and tips that he shared with his guards, but the guards were not to collect the money, probably because he didn't trust them. As soon as the vehicle stopped, Ochoa got out of the passenger front seat, his green boots clearly visible, even though the dusty and dusky night air was oppressively bearing down on them.

Fredo adjusted his lens to get a closeup of the boots and then the man himself, the side of his face, the back of his hair, and his hairline, which contained a large white scar he'd received with a blade of a knife during his incarceration, but it was as telltale as a tattoo on a man. Then when he turned around, Ochoa was chewing on an old cigar, as he was known to only smoke Cubans. His eyes were mean, he had several days growth on his beard, he was fatter than the pictures they'd shown the team earlier, and he appeared to be having some discomfort as he walked. Perhaps his boots were becoming too small for him. His face fashioned a nasty wince. He wore army fatigues, starched and pressed, and a gray shirt probably from his police days. It still sported oak leaf decorations on his pocket with black bars atop his shoulders from earlier days.

One by one, Mr. Ochoa visited each person, reviewed their paperwork, accepted their payments, sometimes in cash. Sometimes it was a note of some kind. One or two people brought bars of gold, which were obvious with their weight and the way they clinked inside the heavy bag as it was lifted to him. All kinds of contraband, including drugs, were turned in to him. Ochoa, when he received drugs, tossed it to his guards, but he accepted it as payment, nonetheless. When he came to the woman and the two children, she sobbed and said something to him, trying to explain a problem. Fredo could barely understand in a dialect, not from Mexico, but possibly El Salvador or Guatemala. It was obvious she was not a woman of means, was short the funds required, and Fredo wished he could record her voice.

"Are you getting this Fredo?" asked Kyle, his LPO.

"Roger that, Sir. I wish I could record it—that's something we must do next time—but she appears to be telling him that she was robbed of her money and she has none."

Fredo's stomach churned as he knew the culprits, but he wasn't sure how this was going to play out for her or her children.

Ochoa grabbed her by the shirt and pulled her face up close to his as he yelled at her that she was a whore and that her need for sex has compromised her life as well as her children's. He screamed at her using several gutter words, and Fredo carefully translated as best he could.

"He's telling her that she is a whore and that because she needed sex, she got robbed. That it was her fault. I think the two gentlemen, one with the one with the green T-shirt over to the left, are the ones who raped her, and I believe they stole from her as well. But she says she does not have the money, and she insists she is not a whore and that she was a victim."

Ochoa slapped her across the face and continued to lecture her, but he let go of her blouse and showed her his forefinger as he screamed back, making the children shudder behind her skirts. One of the earlier migrants who had already paid offered Ochoa to pay her fee and was butt in the stomach by one of the guard's rifles before he could reach Ochoa.

Ochoa seemed to take great care in lecturing her how dangerous it was for her children and that she might have to pay the ultimate price in order for them to go across the border.

Fredo began to translate again. "He asks her to choose which child shall live. He says that he will take her and one child. The other one can live, but she has not paid the fee, and for her services to his guards, he will allow one child to go free."

There were several murmurs and expletives whispered amongst the team. Fredo knew every single man in that unit wanted to just go take them out, and they could, but they didn't have the authorization until they got the verification that it was okay to engage. Things had changed so much in the past five years since they first started working cartels south of the border.

"I should send this up to the shed, Kyle. I think we need to request action. Something is going to happen. Someone is going to die."

"Roger that, Fredo. Send it up. Coop, you get your cellphone out and take some pictures while he's uploading."

Coop used his specially enhanced cellphone, a small gadget he had invented himself. It did not have the confidential link to the head shed that Fredo's did. It took less than thirty seconds before Fredo was back in action.

"Delivered. No acknowledgement yet but delivered."

Fredo continued filming as did Coop, when Kyle

got the ping in his ear.

"It's a no-go. No engagement. Only target is Ochoa. Not the guards, no matter what they've done."

Again, several members of the team swore. Somebody called out for Mother Mary to protect them. Someone else used the name of Jesus. Every single man would give their life for that woman and child, and while Fredo continued to film, he was struck with the fact that he was serving with the finest men he'd ever met in his entire life on this SEAL Team 3. On his team, under such horrible circumstances, the very best of the team came alive. They had the duty to serve and to protect, but only after receiving permission. This wasn't the time to break out and go rogue, ruining all of their careers.

As tensions escalated, the woman pointed to the two men who had raped her, accusing them, and again was beaten to the ground. Before she could clamor up, Ochoa pulled out his pistol and shot her in the head. Several of the women and men in the migrant group screamed and the children began to cry—all the children in the group. The woman's two children stood by but were frozen in shock.

Finally, his little sister collapsed into her ten-year-old brother and appeared to be almost ready to pass out. She was hyperventilating and had gone white as a sheet. She began to vomit, and Ochoa tore her from the arms of the young boy and shot her in the head right between the eyes.

He turned to the boy who looked up at him with wide eyes but who did not flinch. He stood with his chest out, ready to accept the bullet he was sure was going to be his. Fredo had never seen a young migrant child show so much bravery. Ochoa began to lecture him about the lesson he had learned and the fact that his mother had risked her life for him.

The boy nodded. Ochoa leaned into him with a nasty sneer and cocked his ear, putting his hand up to it.

The boy answered, "*Sí, señor.* You are correct. Thank you for my life."

That seemed to move Ochoa slightly. He appeared to soften, smiled tenderly, reached over, though the boy flinched, and tousled his hair. The guards around him unceremoniously dragged the woman and carried the dead child into the jungle where, apparently, she was frisked. One guard returned, holding a cloth bag, which was brought back and dropped at the feet of the boy.

Ochoa barked at the boy, as Fredo translated, "'This is your legacy, now all that is left of your mother.' What an asshole," Fredo added.

He heard several people squeeze their fists together, slip their safeties on and off, and touch their weapons, each one trained on an individual, carefully. If it came to that, they'd all go rogue if Kyle asked them. There would be no hesitation.

Ochoa went down the line and continued collecting his bribes. Another duffel bag of drugs was tossed at his guard's feet, and a squabble ensued about a certain amount of payment received, where a gentleman behind a mother and children paid for their shortfall so they wouldn't have the same outcome. When Ochoa came to the gentleman, he had payment in full, but Ochoa asked for more. Fredo relayed all this to the group. The gentleman said he had no more, but he could deliver some to his relatives waiting on the other side of the border if he would trust him to do so.

What that gentleman got for his efforts was a bullet to the head as well. Fredo was beginning to think that Ochoa routinely killed several of the migrants after he received payment or received mostly all of the payment. In this case, he'd received everything he'd required, but he still wanted to take the man's life. It was like an example to the rest of the group. You only look out for yourself, and if you try to help someone else, it may cost you.

As the man was being dragged off, the woman and three children suffered in silence and looked down at their feet. One of the family members was a teenage young girl, far too pretty to be on this dangerous trip.

Fredo knew they wouldn't get across the border before she was raped multiple times. Not all of the groups suffered this way, but it probably depended on the guards that went with them and where they hooked up.

The line was over, and Ochoa began to pass out money to the guards, of course saving the largest sum for himself. He saved the gold bars and had someone take them to the Humvee, but he passed out dollar bills and peso notes, generously greeted with grins and nods and great approval. He turned to go back to the car.

"Kyle, you've got to get an answer from them."

"I've just relayed the information that he's about to leave. I'm hoping they'll split us up so we can go after him while a few of you follow this group, and we'll catch up later."

Ochoa got into the Humvee and slammed the door.

"Oh, shit. Okay. The answer from above is we follow Ochoa. We grab them, and we bring him over the border. That's our mission. We have to leave the group alone."

Fredo looked at the young boy, who now was missing his younger sister and mother, obviously no money, no skills, and probably no additional resources. He slung the bag over his shoulder and began to walk with the guards. One of the guards was taking a leak behind some bushes and had left his rifle standing nearby.

Fredo grit his teeth. "No, no, no, no, no. Do not do that. Very stupid."

As the Humvee took off, the young boy grabbed the rifle and managed to shoot two of the six guards. Two of the other guards tried to disarm him, and he struggled but finally was beaten to the ground and then shot in the neck. A huge spurt of blood arced across the dusty field. Fredo's heart sank.

The group left him in the clearing to bleed to death, if he wasn't already dead.

Fredo knew Ochoa must have heard the gunshot, but at this point, he'd been paid. He didn't care who died, even if it was one of his own men. He was the cruelest son of a bitch Fredo had ever seen.

The group quickly disappeared into the scrubby forest. Kyle gave the go ahead to follow the tire tracks, and he told the group that a bird was launched so they could get some night vision tracking, and they would figure out a way for them to stop Ochoa before he made it back to his compound.

"May I check on the boy? What if he's still alive?" Fredo asked.

"How are we going to be able to take care of him, Fredo? He's more than likely dead."

"We can try," said Coop. "Let us go check him out. We'll catch up. If I think he can be moved, I'll carry him on my back," said Coop.

"I'll do it too. We'll take turns," said Fredo. Several others on the team stepped forward to agree to the same. They would all take turns carrying the child until proper first aid could be administered if he was alive.

"Okay, Coop, go quickly, but only if you're sure he'll make it."

Cooper, who was their team medic, and Fredo ran to the boy. Cooper searched for a pulse and nodded his head. He'd been shot in the shoulder, not the neck, but it had nicked an artery and he would be bleeding out quickly. Cooper stopped the flow with Fredo's help. They tied off his upper arm with a tourniquet underneath his armpit up to the brachial artery on top of his shoulder.

He tightened it so hard that the boy began to stir, probably from the pain. But he was alive and able to respond, even if slightly.

"I got to tie it tight, otherwise, he won't make it. When he wakes, he's going to be howling. If he makes it that far."

"What do you think? Can we take him?"

"Did you see that kid? He's a fighter. There's no way I'm going to leave a fighter in a jungle after losing his mom and his sister and let him bleed out. No fucking way, Fredo."

"Agreed. So he's going to make it then, right?"

"I will say whatever it takes. And you too."

They picked him up carefully. He had a huge bruise on the left side of his cheek where he had fallen on a rock, but there was no breakage of skin. They saw cuts and bruises on his legs probably from the long trek. And other than that, he was generally malnourished and overly skinny but in fairly good shape.

Cooper fashioned a seat sling so he could be draped over the backside of Coop's tall frame and cinched it around his waist, holding the boy's wrists together, his arms draped over his shoulder, with one hand while he used his other hand to be ready in case he needed his weapon. Fredo carried his medic kit and his communication box, and they ran to catch up to Kyle and the others.

By the time they reached the location where Ochoa was going to approach his campground, it was nearly dark. The compound was well fortified, and their team of twelve would have no luck breaching the doors or getting through the guards. They counted more than fifty armed men. But a further wrinkle was a compound in the middle of the fortress that held some hostages in cages who were being processed. Some were probably held for the lucrative sex trade, others as servants or perhaps being used to negotiate a ransom. But it was not a situation that would get Kyle permission to engage. There would be the possibility of too much innocent loss of life, and there was no verification of the nationalities of the prisoners in the middle of the compound. In other words, no US civilians that could be verified.

Kyle instructed them to make camp and then asked Cooper how the boy was doing.

"He's still alive. I can tell he's breathing but barely, and he peed down my back, which is normal. I'll give him something for pain and get some antibiotics into him for now. I'll set him down and have a good look. Anyway, can we phone something in to pick him up?"

Fredo looked as Kyle shook his head no. "Like I said, if he can't travel with us, then we should have left him back there. I don't want him to cause us to slow down and not be able to get our job done. That's a mistake. I don't want to endanger the team just to save one person, but we'll do what we can, and if there's a way, we'll get him out. I think, at this point, our best…"

"That means we get to steal a vehicle or two," said Fredo.

Several of the others liked the idea and told Kyle so.

"You said they wouldn't allow us to engage, but would they let us steal equipment?" Coop asked.

"I guess if it was considered life or death, anything is possible. We're going to have to wait for the next caravan to get Ochoa. In the meantime, we'll get this kid home, get you guys back, and let's get some better equipment for next time. I say we grab a truck or two, call in some coordinates, and get picked up," whispered Kyle. "And watch out for patrols. We are defenseless if we get spotted."

He sent out two from the team to do reconnaissance, looking for likely vehicles they could easily steal, and hope they could find something that had fuel and was operable.

"I'm going for the Humvee," said Andrew.

"Better not hit the beehive just yet. Just a couple of trucks will do just fine. One if we have to. But make sure they run."

The two SEALs disappeared into the night as Cooper worked on the kid and the rest of the team made camp. Sentry assignments were made by volunteers. They switched everything to night vision and double checked their equipment.

For the first time today, Fredo had hope that something good was about to happen. And he'd been dreading just the opposite all day.

He hoped saving the life of that brave kid would be that something. Right now, after what they'd seen, they needed to experience a miracle. It would be years before he'd get those visions of the deaths out of his head.

CHAPTER 2

SINCE FREDO WAS away on his mission, Mia had received some free tickets to watch the baseball game and took the twins, Diego and Luis, as well as Ricardo, her oldest son. The twins were ten, and Ricardo was thirteen—a gangly preteen boy full of energy, who was an excellent baseball player and all-around athlete.

While Ricardo was athletic like Fredo, his stepdad, the twins were more bookish, which came as a great relief to both Mia and Fredo. After years of trying to get pregnant, they had finally conceived, only to have twins. She had always wanted a girl, but that apparently was not in the cards. And she didn't feel she was made of the right stuff to raise four boys, especially with Fredo being gone so much on missions for SEAL Team 3, so she went back on the pill, and they stopped trying.

Ricardo was tapping drumsticks to everything he could find in the house, wearing his baseball cap backwards, even messing with the twins, tickling them, and joking with them. It was all a result of his excitement over going to the baseball game. The tickets were in a private box space. Someone in the Seal community had been invited but couldn't go, so Mia grabbed the chance to be able to take the boys for free, even though it wouldn't be truly free. They could eat her out of house and home, and she knew it was going to cost her over one hundred dollars just to get them hotdogs and sodas.

In the box seat, food was provided, but they were more the hors d'oeuvre type, so Mia allowed Ricardo to go grab some hot dogs for the three of them. There were ample drinks available, healthy juices and sodas, as well as fresh water, which Mia took advantage of. Several minutes went by.

"Ricardo's been gone an awful long time. I'm hungry," said Luis.

"I'm sure there's quite a line. I wish I could have just ordered it here, and then Ricardo wouldn't miss any of the game. But he'll be back soon. It's only been fifteen minutes," she responded.

At the half hour mark, Mia began to worry. Roughly five minutes later, Ricardo entered the box, sheepishly holding several hotdogs, with mustard and ketchup smeared onto his T-shirt. He looked like he was out of breath and apologized. His face and hairline sweated profusely. Mia took a damp towel and dabbed his forehead and cheeks. He was bright red.

"What did you do? You ran the whole way back or something?" she asked him.

Ricardo was rather glum and rolled his left shoulder, like Fredo did on many occasions, and bashfully told her he was just hurrying to get back. And he was sorry it took so long.

The boys were happy with their dogs as they watched the rest of the ballgame, Mia paying more attention to her boys and how they cheered and shouted with the other guests in the box suite than the baseball game. In fact, if Fredo were to ask her, she wouldn't have remembered the score. But one thing she noticed was that Ricardo seemed to be affected by something, and was more quiet than she'd expected. She suspected something had happened in his adventure to get food for his little brothers.

After the game, she thanked the box holder for donating the tickets and spoke to her and her husband for several minutes, indicating that Fredo would be very happy to learn about their generosity.

Mrs. Johansen gave her a hug. "Oh my dear, it's the least we could do. After all, he's out there fighting for you and me. I think a little fun day with his wife and kids is entirely in order. Your boys are growing up strong, Mia. Very handsome young men," Mrs. Johansen said, winking.

"I'm very proud of them. And, of course, I'm proud of Fredo too." Mia blushed, trying to suppress her embarrassment.

She said her goodbyes to the rest of the group while she shepherded her three boys out of the box seat rows, down the hallway, and into the general population of fans leaving for the parking lots. She noticed Ricardo was searching his surroundings frequently as if looking for someone, and this alerted Mia to the fact that she was going to have to sit him down and have a discussion out of the ears of Diego and Luis. He didn't seem to connect with anyone in particular or notice anything in particular, so she wasn't alarmed, but he didn't stop searching, turning around and looking up and down the lines of people as they made their way out into the parking lot, until he sat in the car and she began to leave, which automatically locked the doors. Ricardo leaned back in his seat, his arms folded across his chest, closed his eyes, and was asleep in mere minutes.

When they got home, the boys were sent upstairs to shower and get ready for bed, while Mia asked Ricardo to join her in the kitchen.

"Have a seat. I want to talk to you about something," she said to her son.

Ricardo's expression was one of wide-eyed disbelief, and then he added a shrug and deposited his lanky frame in the chair at their breakfast table. He didn't make eye contact but focused on his hands folded on the Formica top.

"You want some milk or some ice water? Or some fruit juice, Ricardo?"

"Just some water, I guess. Are you upset about something, Mom?"

"No. Not at all," Mia lied. "I just want to have a little talk about something. I'll be right there."

She poured a tall glass of ice water for both of them and sat at a 45-degree angle to her son, placing the two glasses on metal coasters. She watched him take a long drink and set the glass down, but still avoid eye contact.

She prayed for strength, hoping she could extract the information she sought without causing a scene.

"I can tell when something's happened, Ricardo. And I do believe something happened today. I don't want to guess, and I don't want to worry, but you seemed disheveled and preoccupied with something after you came back. I would like you to tell me the truth about what went on today."

He looked startled for a minute before gaining composure to answer her.

"Nothing. I mean, there was just a lot of people, that's all. It was hard to find a place where there wasn't a line that was going to take an hour to get through, but I finally did, and by the time you order and then it gets given to you and you put all the fixings on, it just took longer than I expected. Thank goodness I didn't have to get a soda."

"Ricardo, I mean it. I want the straight scoop. I need to know what went on. And don't tell me nothing did. Your mother has a sixth sense about these things, and I'm especially alerted to danger or negative things. Something happened. You need to tell me now. Or when your dad gets home, he'll be all over your case about it. I think you'd much rather talk to me than to Fredo. Is that right?"

Ricardo took another long sip on his ice water, chewing an ice cube with a crushing jaw motion. He swallowed and set the glass back down. He began to nod his head. "Okay, you're not going to want to hear it."

"All the more reason you should tell me. Come on, Ricardo. You know I'm doing this for you, for all of us. I don't like to be left out of something important. And if it's something that's got you upset, I need to know about it."

"Do you know that Caesar, my sperm donor, is getting out of prison?" After his comment, he chanced a look at Mia's face and probably got the expression he was expecting. Mia was truly thrown off guard with this reveal.

"How do you know this?"

"I ran into a couple of guys. They told me." Again, Ricardo looked down at his hands, at the glass, anywhere but up at Mia's face. He didn't want to make eye contact.

Mia leaned forward, and she grabbed Ricardo's wrist in her palm, begging for him to look up. "Who are these guys?"

"They're kids, like me. Except their dads are in the Scorpions. These guys are newbies, wannabes. Assholes, really."

Mia withdrew her hand and stared at the ceiling, wondering what in the world had been created today. She missed not having Fredo around, and she was devastated with this news. She wondered whether the boys sought Ricardo out or, which would be worse, he sought them out. She hoped to God he answered her question the way she wanted. She had to ask.

"So you started the conversation then?"

"Nah, like I said, they're assholes. They're delinquents. In and out of school, you know. They're headed in their father's footsteps. But they like to make trouble, and they pick on people. They like to pick on the weak ones."

Now Mia understood why Ricardo didn't want to tell her. Was he ashamed he was considered weak?

"Well, not exactly fair, especially when there's more

than one of them and there's only one of you, is that correct?"

"Yes. There were four. And I guess their dads and older brothers are big and important in the gang. They asked me if I wanted to check it out, and I told them hell no. Then they asked me again if I wanted to meet my father, my sperm donor, but I told them no. I already had a father. And I mean it too, Mom. I have no desire to meet him. And I didn't know what to do so I pretended that I was going along with things. Until they started hassling me. They ordered a couple more hot dogs and soda and some candy, so that the guy taking the order added their order to mine. I decided not to protest and just paid for it, and I'll reimburse you out of my allowance, but it was an extra twenty bucks or more."

"You did the right thing. The best thing is not to escalate. And I'm glad you told them you didn't want to have anything to do with Caesar, but you need to keep your distance from these guys."

"Yeah, except they're at school, and they're bullies. I mean, that's all they do. The administration doesn't do a damn thing about it. They're handling all these kids with kid gloves. It's not fair on the rest of us, but I don't want to make waves."

"Well, I'm glad you told me, Ricardo. And you are very brave to do so. You stay away from those boys, and let's sit down and talk about it when your dad gets home. I think it should be pretty soon now. Christy called me to let me know they were on their way. I'm sure Fredo's going to want to know about it."

"Mom, I don't want Dad getting involved, because with his job and everything, he could get in trouble."

"Thank you for that, Ricardo, but you know your dad would do anything to protect you. If it was required, he'd be there for you."

"I know that. I also know that I have no desire to become one of their newbies or to have any kind of a relationship with the asshole who got you pregnant. I look at him as being pure trash. I just hope there's not as much of him in me and more of you. And I hope he doesn't want or pursue finding me. That makes me uncomfortable, Mom."

Mia stood from her chair, came around the side of the table, and gave Ricardo a hug, kissing him on the cheek. "You are so special to me, Ricardo. I will not let anything happen to you. You need to be honest and tell me everything that happens regarding these boys. Don't underestimate their evil. You know your dad is working on cartel business down in Mexico, and these guys here in San Diego are like cartel-lite, wannabe gangsters, but they cause a lot of havoc. Given the chance, they could be dangerous. At some point, we're going to have to tell your administrators that you've been harassed. But not yet. We'll talk to Fredo first."

"Okay. Thanks, Mom. Can I go now?"

"Of course."

Ricardo stood and, even at thirteen, was nearly as tall as Mia was. He gave her a chaste hug, not a needy one, just enough to show his developing affection for the human race, and she knew he didn't want to appear weak. Mia hugged him back harder and then let him go, watching him run upstairs.

The twins were showering together and probably making a huge mess in the bathroom, judging from all the sounds they were making. Under the circumstances, Mia decided to let Ricardo sort it out. In a few short moments, she heard him lay down the law, and Diego and Luis were muted.

She smiled to herself. He sounded just like Fredo.

CHAPTER 3

THE TWO SEALs assigned to stealing a vehicle were able to hot-wire a covered personnel carrier, and the ride across the border area—over three hundred fifty miles, plus or minus along the Texas border alone—was bumpy, hot, and extremely dusty. It was also one of the most dangerous parts of Mexico, not only for Americans or American soldiers, but Mexican citizens as well.

The goal was, even though they would have to travel a great deal in Mexico, to cross the border at a large designated area as close as possible to San Diego, close to their Team base, where they could have their State/Homeland liaison meet them, rather than a remote outpost elsewhere. It was going to take them nearly eight hours to make the journey.

Of course, everyone on the team was worried about the survival of the child.

Just outside of San Diego proper, after having driven most of the night, the sun was beginning to show a pink-orange-peachy glow. They'd arranged to meet the Department of Homeland Security liaison, who was also a State Department special agent, who could take them from Mexico and, with his badge, get them through the border crossing with the child without questions being asked.

Kyle and Fredo had relayed all of Fredo's photographs, as well as some of Coop's, identified the sighting of Ochoa, and were told their intel agencies were still trying to determine when the next trip would be, but that it probably would be soon.

There were changes going on within the US State Department, and those changes were going to have an effect on the size of the migrant caravans, as well as who would be coming. The State Department was interested in the fact that this particular group was made up mostly of women and children. That was not usually the case. More and more, it was becoming solid groups of military-age males, some with apparent military training or former police training, and although they didn't have anything specific to point to, the SEALs were told that those groups were indeed extremely dangerous. In fact, State told Kyle they were starting to view these groups as armed militia successfully getting across the border and hiding out in Texas and Arizona. It was a new game, all the same players, but the heat level had ratcheted up tremendously.

The boy moaned occasionally, and Coop moni-
tored him carefully to make sure he didn't overdose
him but needed him comfortable so he wouldn't go
into shock. His pulse was getting better, and he had
been given fluids intravenously, so his organs and body
could stabilize and generate the additional blood he
needed to heal. But he was far from well, and it
wouldn't take long for a huge infection to not only take
over his upper shoulder region, but it was close to his
heart, his lungs, the blood flow to his brain. It was not
looking good, but he was stable for now.

As agreed, their liaison, Carlos Gutierrez, met them
at the little villa in Mexicali, a safe house for State
Department's special agents from time to time. Since
the truck was without call letters, even without a
license, they were not easily identified, but the fact that
it was a large truck and could carry some twenty men
made them a target anyway. Kyle was able to relay all
this information to the State Department, and
Gutierrez brought a California license plate and new
registration papers for the truck to hand to the border
guards.

"Glad to see you, Gutierrez. This wasn't the plan,"
said Kyle to the agent, who had sweated through his
white shirt, making it stick to his torso.

Gutierrez pulled back the canvas flap and examined

the child. "He's awfully white. You sure he's still alive?"

"He is. But he's going to need surgery right away," said Coop.

Fredo placed his hand on the boy's forehead, searching for signs he could be picking up a fever, and actually, the boy felt clammy and cold. He didn't know whether to feel good about that or not. But Fredo knew it wasn't normal, and the sooner he could get medical treatment in a sterile situation, the better.

Gutierrez continued. "Okay then. I'm going to hop a ride with you and leave my car here. I'm going to need to be driving when I get to the border. They aren't going to listen to you, and they aren't going to want to bribe me, so that's the way it's got to be. Anything I need to know about this vehicle?" Gutierrez asked Kyle, who had been driving.

"If it's all the same to you, I'd like to go shotgun," said Kyle.

"Fine by me. But we're going to be speaking Spanish. Try to keep up." The salty agent gave Kyle a cheesy grin.

"*Sí, sí.* I got you." Kyle continued, "She sticks a little bit going from second to third, maybe there's going to be a future issue with the transmission. I'm just guessing they don't service these things. And it's been out in the hot desert probably more days than it's been in the jungle, but either one is a truck destroyer. I doubt they ever change the oil either. Every available man in Ochoa's camp carries an AK-47 and a side arm. I doubt any of them are mechanics."

"Thanks for the heads-up. I've got Scripps on my phone here, and I'm going to let your medic do a video call with them so they can be ready for the kid." He handed the phone to Coop, and immediately, Fredo heard the crew from the ER on the line.

"What's going to happen with him?" Fredo asked Gutierrez. "You know that he witnessed the death of his mother and little sister. She was only about three years old. I don't know if he has any relatives in the rest of the group, nobody he paid attention to before she was shot. But what happens to a kid like this?"

The agent shrugged. "He'll be processed. It's going to take a while. He'll probably be placed in a foster care situation if we can find one. There are NGOs that are picking up these kids, but we're being careful to make sure they aren't funneled right back into the hands of the people that kidnapped them or caused their injuries all over again. And that's happened a lot unfortunately."

"I think every man here would help with the care of this kid," Kyle added. "But I don't know what the State Department's stance is on it. You'll let us know, though, right?"

"You bet. I'm just a phone call away. And if I'm not

answering, well, then it means I'm south of the border doing something I can't reveal my location by phone. I will make sure to mention to my upper tier your concerns."

Gutierrez had his phone returned and then walked to the front of the truck. Fredo followed the two until he realized there wasn't room for three in the front seat.

"Will we be able to see him?" he asked.

That drew an inquisitive look from Kyle.

"You've kind of formed an attachment to this kid, Fredo," Kyle added.

A shout came from the back of the transport. "All this is nice chit-chat, but we got to get this kid to a hospital and fast," yelled Coop. "Let's dispense with the niceties and get him in the US of A. I just don't want to be doing a fire fight with him in the back."

"Roger that." Kyle handed Gutierrez the keys. "It's all yours, Sport. Don't get a speeding ticket or we'll all go to jail." Fredo headed to the rear, but not before he heard the agent give a smart retort.

"Not a chance in hell that it's going to happen." Gutierrez reached in his back pocket and brought out a huge gold badge. It wasn't lost on Kyle that the big letters rounding the top of the badge said special agent. State Department of the United States of America on the bottom. Even from a distance, the letters stood out like they were neon.

"That must be a get out of jail card then. Will that hold for all of us?" he asked.

"I have the full backing of the United States of America. They don't fuck with these. Trust me. Even the low lives don't fuck with these."

Fredo hopped in the back. The truck had already started moving so he got a couple hands up and then plunked himself near Coop.

Barely five minutes later, they were stopped in a long line of cars coming to one of the largest points of entry in the United States. Gutierrez moved the truck out of the line and advanced, coming up to a kiosk and stopping briefly before exiting the truck. Immediately, several semi-automatics were trained on him. He quickly got his badge out.

While Kyle and everyone else tried to listen, Gutierrez was speaking rapidly, waving his arms and pointing back at the truck. The sentry called for permission, and soon, a senior official with several colorful metals over his breast pocket advanced on them, listened to Gutierrez's narration, slowly studied the truck, and then glanced back to Gutierrez. After some further discussion, he nodded, and a barricade was removed so the truck could advance through to the US side. As the truck began to rev up, everyone in the back breathed the sigh of relief. Fredo's peephole in the canvas soon showed nothing but road and cactus. Several others used holes in the canvas cover to look at the situation they had just left.

"Thank God. It worked." And then louder, T.J. shouted to the front, "You're all right there, Carlos. Hey, do you have an extra one of those I could borrow sometime?"

It was time for some levity, and several of the guys chuckled. Coop was still attending the boy. Fredo used a cold pack on his forehead, around his cheeks, and especially around the bruise near his eye. The bruise was getting huge and quite purple, but other than that, his lips were red and his coloring was beginning to pink up a bit. It was an improvement.

In twenty minutes, they were at Scripps, Coop had relayed the kid's vitals to the team, and a crash cart and gurney were all prepped for them as soon as they drove up to the emergency room. Fredo counted two doctors and four nurses or orderlies, who quickly picked the boy up, placed him on the gurney, kept the drip going for his fluids, and ran, literally raced through the emergency room doors down the hallway toward what Fredo knew was going to be the surgical center.

Coop shook his head. "Lucky kid. Just under a lucky star. Of course, you saw how he reacted," he said to Fredo.

Fredo nodded yes.

"No kid should have to see that, and I'm sure as hell glad she didn't see the death of her daughter. I just don't understand why these people risk so much. They must have been sold a bill of goods about how safe it was. If they only knew what the numbers were. It's awful," said Gutierrez. "I'm going to go inside and fill out the paperwork and get some things started. Kyle, you want to come in and give your information in case he wakes up and I get permission for you guys to visit him?"

"That would be awesome. He has a lot of information—where they started from, who the men were, maybe even their names or who some of the migrants were. I'd like to get that information from him so we could use that on the next stop. I'd be most grateful if you'd allow that, Sir," said Kyle.

"We're all on the same team here. He's one lucky kid."

"That he is," said Fredo. "And again, sir, I want you to know that there'd probably be a line in this team here of people who would agree to help take care of him. If he needs a sponsor, one of us could probably do it. In fact, we'd probably have to fight each other over it."

Gutierrez laughed at that. "Well, at least if that's the way it goes, we'd be pretty sure he wouldn't be trafficked or sent back to Mexico. Not unless he's a child murderer."

"You're still doing the DNA testing?" asked Coop.

"We are. But not officially. And you didn't hear that from me. We have to have a database, otherwise we don't know what we got. And of course it's not enough to do disease or health testing, but at least we can tell familial strains and perhaps find somebody here in the United States that he's related to. But you're going to have to question him with me there. I don't think they'll let you talk to him by yourself."

"We'll abide by the rules, sir," Kyle said.

Fredo elected to stay behind and talk to the boy in case he was conscious, so he placed a call to Mia and had to leave a message. He figured she was still asleep.

He gave his information to the emergency room and made sure the comment was left that the boy had intel that was going to be most valuable to their job following up and attempting to deal with the coyotes and the cartel members. He didn't want that noted in the kid's file because there was no control over who looked at his records, but he let the head nurse in on the importance that they get a chance to talk to him quickly. But nothing that would interfere with his health.

Fredo and Gutierrez sat in the surgery waiting room. He'd never met someone from Homeland so senior, and he asked Gutierrez how he managed to get his job.

"That's a long and tangled story. I was on a gang task force in Northern California, San Jose area. That's in Silicon Valley."

"I know where it is. So you were a local cop or Feds?"

"SJPD. Anyway, we kept seeing the same things over and over again—kids recruited, especially young males who were too young to go to jail but would get off with lighter sentences. Some were mules, bringing in contraband. But more and more, that part was ending since that was more or less for small timers. Now they were coming in with trucks and planes and boats. It's gotten a hundred times worse than when I first started. So the real contraband now with the border crossings is the human trafficking. These girls are sold, convinced that all they have to do is work a year in a rich family's home with glossy photos that they show them. I've seen those photos. Those assholes. And they get parents introducing them to their daughters willingly and letting them come, thinking that they're sending them to a better life. It's a shame. And it's hard to get ahold of, especially these kids that come from the small villages where internet and TVs are spotty. There are always tales of people who came back to small villages rich and rolling in dough. All it takes is a few of those people, and suddenly, the whole town wants to go. It's a shame," Gutierrez said, shaking his head.

"So how'd you get with the State Department from the gang task force?" Fredo asked.

"I had a buddy from high school who got into doing border guard duty for Homeland Security. Unfortunately, they found him way out in the middle of the desert somewhere, executed. He'd been tortured too. It broke my heart, but I was furious. I wanted to kill someone. I mean really kill someone. I didn't think I was going to be calm enough to go back to my police duties, so I applied through Homeland Security for a special agent job. I didn't want to be driving migrants across the border, changing diapers, and feeding babies. I wanted to go after the criminals, and I wanted to have the kind of authority where I could really do something. The problem with my police work was all our efforts were interfered with, depending on the jurisdiction. We have such a wide variety of judges and district attorneys… it depends on where the busts happened. Sometimes they'll plead they're from a different locale, and you have to use something outside of San Diego or San Jose or maybe way up in the mountains. We get a change of venue all the time. And I'd have to drive all over hell and back to these court cases, and most of them, we lost. And guys that were set to be deported just disappeared on us. I wasn't doing anything. I mean, the percentage of guys we caught and actually deported was tiny compared to the amount that got through. I just couldn't work there anymore and see the numbers rising, see the carnage, and not have the authority to fix some small part of it."

Fredo knew Gutierrez was one of the white hats, a good guy, like his SEAL buddies.

"Well, that's kind of why I joined the SEAL teams. Same thing. Difference is we do ops with multiple men, and each guy would die for me. We don't always achieve our goal, but we know how to keep each other safe, and we know we can depend on each other. It's a group thing, not an individual thing. It's dangerous to do it on your own. But I think we are a force for good. Otherwise, well, the risks are too great, and now that I've got a wife and three kids, she needs me home. Now more than ever."

"Sounds like you have your priorities straight. If I wasn't so old, shoot, I would've become a SEAL. Or tried to. I don't know if I could have passed everything, though. You guys are iron men."

"Nah," Fredo sighed. Then he smiled and stared right back at Gutierrez. "We just don't quit. We're dumb like that."

The surgery took well over two hours, and it was nearly noon when a doctor walked slowly down the hallway and gave them the news.

"He might actually lose his arm. Whoever tied that tourniquet did a hell of a good job stopping the bleeding, but man, he damaged that tissue. We have a collapsed artery we had to repair and all kinds of other things going on, but if we can get that circulation going, he'll be okay. I'm surprised it didn't nick anything else. I mean, there's all kinds of stuff there in his chest. I think it ricocheted off his clavicle, because we got a fracture there, and if it had gone the wrong way, shoot, it could have gone to his spine. But I think he'll make it. He's pretty strong. He's a fighter."

Fredo was relieved. "Thank God. So is he put in a coma? Is that what the next step is?"

"No, I think he's stable enough to get some painkillers, but we're going to have to go in again probably in a day or two just to make sure he's doing well enough, and we'll have to repair that clavicle and check on our other work. I don't want any bleeders going on. We'll get his vitals and just track him for a while, but he's going to have to have a couple of surgeries. I'm glad you brought him here, because I don't think many of the emergency rooms down here could have handled it," the doctor answered.

"Thanks, Doc," Gutierrez said as he shook his hand.

"He's going to need a lot of care. Some physical therapy and, if he loses that arm, prosthetics. It's going to be a long haul for him. We'll see how he goes if he wakes up, if he's cooperative, and if you can convince him to be cooperative, it'll go a lot better for him. Does he have any next of kin?"

"That's just it, Doctor. He witnessed the murder of his mother and his three-year-old sister. That was hard to watch. And he tried to kill the guys that did it, and that's how he got injured. He was home free—he could have just stayed with the group, but he fought back. So yeah, he is a fighter."

"Well, he's lucky then."

"We've all been saying that. He's the luckiest little kid around. At least for today. Until the next time we find one. And that'll probably happen soon."

CHAPTER 4

MIA AND HER mother, Felicia Guzman-Mayfield, were making fresh tortillas and tamales in Felicia's newly remodeled kitchen. It was something she'd enjoyed doing many times during the year, something she and her mother started when Mia was barely walking. Her mother would put her in a highchair and give her some dough to roll out, even giving her dull knives to have her chop tomatoes and other ingredients for the tamales Felicia was famous for.

Mia figured it would be nice to give Fredo a nice home-cooked traditional meal, since tonight he would be home. It also gave her the stability, standing next to her mother for nearly a half day, gaining strength and courage to discuss with Fredo the reveal about Caesar's possible release. Felicia had that quiet courage, forged through many years of adversity in Puerto Rico, when Mia's father was still alive. Now, Felicia was loved again, this time by Gus Mayfield, her second husband.

"You enjoyed the baseball game, yes?" Felicia asked her.

Mia was hesitant to answer, not wanting to engage her mother further with some of her concerns, especially since she hadn't talked to Fredo yet.

"They loved it, and I enjoyed it because I loved watching their faces. It was very generous of them to donate those tickets. We had private box seats in a suite area, catered. Oh, there was good wine and all kinds of fresh fruit smoothies. It was delightful. Hardly felt like a baseball game though. My recollections of baseball games were sitting in the sun, getting sunburned, and dropping mustard all the way down the front of my chest."

Felicia laughed. "Your father loved taking you to soccer games in Puerto Rico. He wanted you to play soccer, football, you remember, Mia?"

"I'm not an athlete, Mother. I don't like getting bruised and muddy. Some of my friends in school were banshees about football. I didn't want to get my clothes or my hair or my makeup messed up. It's amazing that I even married a man of action."

"Well, that's because he was one of your brother's best friends on SEAL Team 3. You met him through Armando."

"How could I forget? He reminds me every time I see him."

Felicia smiled and paused, before adding, "Armando is doing better these days. Sambra has brought some new life to his eyes. He's not all the way over Gina's loss, but I think, in time, he will settle down. Sambra wants to have children, and I think Armando's a little bit concerned since he and Gina had had so much trouble. He's worried that she could be too fragile."

"Oh, these men. These team guys all think we're so darn fragile and we're going to break if they squeeze us too hard. We're just as strong as they are in other ways, and we endure so much. I just don't get where men have to treat us like we're porcelain teacups or something. It sort of annoys me. The fact is, we can handle a lot more stress and pain than the men can. And some of them, I have it on good authority, faint at the sight of blood. Can you imagine that?"

"Oh, no. Who?"

"Well, I know this new guy Crane, he did. Plus, at their in-doc session, he fainted when he got a shot. It's so funny. These big macho guys can do so much, but the sight of blood or needles drives some crazy."

"Well, I'm sure if Crane is married—"

"No, he's not. But I know what you're going to say."

"Yes, he will never make it in a delivery room, will he?" Mrs. Guzman answered.

"Nope. And he shouldn't even try."

They worked in silence until Felicia's husband, Gus Mayfield, entered the kitchen.

"Oh my gosh, it smells heavenly in here. Do I have a couple of Puerto Rican angels stirring up some kind of a heavenly dish for me tonight?" Mayfield had been a detective and lived alone after his unhappy marriage and divorce. Felicia's husband had been killed in the line of duty in Puerto Rico, and she never remarried after she came to the United States with her two children, Armando and Mia. Their love match was something Mia and all the rest of the wives from SEAL Team 3 were touched by. Big huge Mayfield treated Felicia like she admired her prized plate-sized dahlias in her front yard.

"That's what we are, Gus. Angels. Fredo gets back today, so I thought I'd give him a little treat. But there's going to be plenty for you, don't worry about it. And my boys love tamales as well. In fact, I think the twins could eat them for breakfast, lunch and dinner."

"I don't see anything wrong with that." Gus came over and gave Mia a peck on her cheek, wrapping his arm around her shoulder. He was careful not to get any of the cornmeal on the sleeve of his shirt or his protruding belly.

"So Fredo's been gone for—how long were they gone for?" asked Mayfield.

"This one was a short op. They're after cartel bosses

who are trafficking women and children at the border. I think he left three weeks ago Sunday. But they're done, and Christy told me they'd be back today."

"They get their man?" Mayfield asked.

"I'm not sure. I wait for Fredo to tell me. If it's important. But you know they usually do."

Just then, Mia's cell phone rang. It was Fredo.

"Hey, sweetheart. I'm sitting in an empty house," Fredo barked.

"Well, the boys are in school. It's only two o'clock. I pick them up in a half an hour, unless you want to."

"I'll do that. So where have you been all day? I've been trying to reach you for two hours."

Mia looked at her phone and noted that he had left several messages. "I'm sorry, you're right. I don't understand. We must have been in the store, or we were out in the garden. I must have left the phone inside and missed your calls. Not intentional. I'm not avoiding you. I have something special for you tonight."

"Well, does it involve getting naked and swimming in the pool?" Fredo asked.

"Remember, Fredo, we have three boys. And I haven't yet shown them what I look like naked. I don't think you want me to do that, or did I get it wrong?"

Mayfield and Felicia laughed.

"So you're at your mom's house? What the hell are

you doing there?"

"That's your surprise. And you're going to love it."

"Okay, so I'll get the boys. Do you need me to pick up anything at the store?"

"Nope, I'm almost done here, and then I'll be home in about forty-five minutes to an hour. Make sure the boys get started on their homework right away. I know Ricardo has a report due early next week. I doubt he's done enough research."

"Will do."

Mia signed off and sighed. She knew it was a good idea to cook Fredo a special dinner, which would allow them to linger together while the boys go for a quick swim and then head to bed early. That would give her the time she needed to explain to Fredo what had happened yesterday. She decided to quiz Mayfield about it.

"Gus, I received some disturbing news yesterday. It seems Caesar is going to be released from prison. I was under the impression he got a thirty-year sentence. Do you know what's going on?" she asked him.

Mayfield's face elongated with a worried wrinkle in his forehead. All of a sudden Mia thought he looked ten years older.

"I have my contacts, but no, I didn't hear that. I don't think anybody on your legal team knows it either, because weren't they supposed to call you if he got early release?"

"They're supposed to. I haven't seen anything in the news, not that it would be news, but you know with his reputation and the gang so active, even more active now that he was behind bars, I just am not very happy. If you could, I'd like it if you could look into it a little bit for me. I didn't get many details."

"Wait. Where'd you get this intel from?"

Mia didn't want to tell him it was Ricardo and also didn't want to tell her stepfather about the confrontation with Ricardo. Eventually, it was going to have to come out, but she wanted to discuss it with Fredo first. That was always a rule for them. Their family came first, and then by agreement, they could share it outside the family. The release of Caesar might be a hoax, so she didn't think it was inappropriate to tell Mayfield.

"I'm not at liberty, since I'm not sure the information's accurate. But if you wouldn't mind checking into it, if you can, that would help. I want to talk to Fredo first. I'll let you know. But I'd like to get it verified. Would you do that for me?"

"Of course, Sweetheart. I could make some calls right now if you like."

"Gus," Felicia started. "Why don't you do that, while we're finishing up here and putting everything away. I think it would be a good idea for Mia to have that information before she sits down to talk to Fredo."

Mayfield mumbled something as he left the room and headed for his office located in the back bedroom of the little house.

"Is he upset, Mom?" Mia asked.

"No, he's just tired. All the years and all the tragedies he saw, it wears on him. And he's going to worry about this Caesar thing. Let's hope it's false information, okay?"

"I agree with that. But something tells me, with the money and the people in his organization, he can afford to get himself out of jail somehow. I just don't know how he does it."

The kitchen was clean, and the tamales were placed in a glass baking square with a plastic snapping lid for easy transportation home. The dishwasher was turned on, and the kitchen towels were tossed in the washing machine. Mrs. Guzman took Mia's apron from her, added her own to the handful, and dropped them in the washing machine, turning it on. Her last act as kitchen monitor was to sweep the kitchen floor. Mia held the dustpan.

Mayfield came in just as Mia was coming back from making a second trip to her car, loading up supplies. He had a pensive expression on his face. It wasn't a happy one. Mia braced for something she knew she wasn't going to like.

"Well, I've just talked to the warden over at the county facility. He verified that Caesar got an appeal, and his conviction was overturned, partially on the testimony of somebody who confessed to the murder. I'm not sure how he could get around all the other charges, the kidnapping, the brutal treatment you had at his hand, but it's probably easy for people to recant since that's what the gang does, they intimidate. It's probably more a case that without the murder charge he'd get off quickly with the other charges anyway, so probably better to just release him. The warden says the state can always recharge him, but he doesn't think they will."

"So he's already out then?" Mia asked. She looked at her mother, who was standing next to Mayfield, her palm over her mouth.

"It appears that's true, Mia. I'm sorry to say, if he wants to, he has the right to see Ricardo. I'm not sure what your standing's going to be, but you probably better plan on getting a good attorney and taking some precautions."

Mia's eyes teared up. "Well, I'm going to go home and have this nice dinner. I'm going to greet my husband and watch my kids play outside. I'm going to have a tall sangria, and then I'll face the music. It's been a delightful afternoon over here. I'm so glad you were available, Mom. We'll have to do it again. I needed this."

Felicia melted, stepping close so she could take Mia in her arms. She spoke to her in little cooing sounds whispering little things in her ear, just like she always had done.

"Well, the good thing is she's married to a Navy SEAL. And he's got a lot of buddies, and she couldn't be in better hands. I'd offer to have you guys stay over here, but the house is so small, and I actually think you're safer with Fredo. But if he has to leave again quickly, I'll help you make some other arrangements."

"Christy Lansdowne will probably have a say in that, Dad."

"Of course. I forgot about that." He gave her a brisk smile. "Somehow, we'll figure it out. But don't you hesitate to let me know if you need anything. I'll probably get some more information later on, and if it's important, I'll call you. But otherwise, I'm not going to spoil his first evening home with you. Just try to relax and forget about it. We can always deal with this tomorrow."

Mia stepped up to her stepdad, wrapped her arms around his neck, and allowed herself to be enveloped in his huge arms.

"Thank you, Dad. I love you."

"Me too, Kid. Me too."

CHAPTER 5

FREDO PICKED UP all three boys at St. Cecilia School. The twins came out first, and then Ricardo showed up at the parking lot, coming from the gym. Everybody had their backpacks stuffed with books. The twins had checked theirs out from the library, and Ricardo had brought home a large encyclopedia borrowed from his history teacher.

"Boy, you guys have some homework. Ricardo, you are using this for your report?"

"Yup. I got to do some work before the weekend. Otherwise, I don't think I can finish it in time."

As Fredo took their backpacks and loaded them in the back of his Hummer, the three boys sat as they usually did, Ricardo in front and Luis and Diego in the second seat.

"We good to go? Anybody need to get something on the way home?" Fredo asked them. He wasn't expecting a huge celebration since this wasn't one of their long ops. The boys had gotten quite used to the routine of Fredo being gone maybe eight or ten times during the year. Not like in the old days when he would be gone for three or four months. Many things about the SEAL community had changed over the years. This was easier on the families, doing short trips usually lasting no more than two weeks or a month at the most.

"I'm good," said Diego. Luis agreed. Ricardo shook his head and didn't say anything.

"Okay, well, I think your mother has something special planned. I'm not quite sure what it is, but she was over at your grandmother's house today."

"That means a nice dinner." Ricardo said. "That's what she does when she goes over to Granny's house. They cook. They talk and they cook. And they gossip and they cook. And they tell stories, exaggerations, and they cook."

Fredo grinned. "Yup, that's my Mia. She is a mother's daughter."

The boys came racing through the front door as soon as they arrived. Mia stepped outside to give Fredo a big hug. She even offered to carry his duty bag.

"No can do, sweetheart. Rules. I got rules. Now, what's this surprise?" he said as he kissed her on both cheeks and then gave her a quick kiss on the lips. He studied her face, which caused him to ask the question,

"Are you okay?"

"Yes, but there is something we have to talk about. I'll do it after dinner, after the boys go down. But we have to talk, Fredo."

"Is this bad news?"

"I'm not sure. Please," she put her palms on Fredo's shoulders, "please, let's just have an early dinner, let them play in the pool, and then you and I can have that talk. Don't try to get it out of me. I really don't want to do this in front of the kids."

"Should I be worried?"

"Fredo, I told you, I don't want to do this right now. I want to wait until after dinner."

"Can I bribe you?"

"You're impossible. If I tell you what it is, it's going to ruin your dinner."

"Well, then, you have to tell me now. There's no more getting out of it. What is it?"

She looked at her feet. "Caesar has been released from jail." She searched his face, reading him like a book.

Fredo stared back at her, watching her beautiful brown eyes now tearing up and tears overflowing down her cheeks. He was flabbergasted. "How the hell did that happen?"

"We don't know. When I was at my mom's, I asked Gus if he could make a call or two, verify that information."

"Wait a minute. Where did you get the infor-mation, Mia?"

"Well, it gets worse, Fredo. Ricardo was confronted at school, and one of the boys in some of his classes, they're acquaintances of his, are younger brothers or sons of Caesar's gang members. They told him. And they told him that he wanted to see Ricardo. I don't know if that's true. I think they just tried to scare him. But Ricardo is quite upset about it. As he should be. So Caesar is released, and we got it confirmed by the warden. Gus said he'll help us however he can, but he suggested that we get an attorney. Perhaps—and this came from the boys again—perhaps Caesar is going to try to make a play to get partial custody of Ricardo. I don't know the first thing about that, so we're going to have to game up, right?"

Fredo was staring at the ground, feeling the insides of his stomach churning, helpless, lost as to what to do. He knew it wouldn't be wise to just pick everybody up and leave, leave his job and all the other team guys behind. He knew the best thing would be if somehow Caesar was rearrested and recharged. And now it was his time, his turn to do some research.

"Mia, well, I'm glad you told me. I'm going to put it out of my mind for a little while until we get through dinner. Thank you for letting me know. I'm going to sit with it a bit, and maybe I'll have some better ideas in an hour or two. Gosh, I was so looking forward to just going to bed early and being in your arms. I can't help but feel that Caesar is going to want to come between us. I'm not going to let that happen."

"But you better not do something stupid, Fredo. I can't have you arrested or out of the picture. It's too dangerous. I need you by my side. I know, together, we can make it work."

Fredo had been planning on broaching the subject to Mia about them adopting the little boy he'd rescued in Mexico, whose name was Ivan. He learned that later after the boy's admission. Now that was going to definitely take a backseat to this new wrinkle. The easiest solution would also be the most devastating. Fredo hoped Caesar would get involved in some kind of a gangland shootout, fall down, and never arise again. But that would be too perfect and something not likely to happen. But he knew also that people like Caesar who were bullies, only spoke truth to power. Unless Caesar knew Fredo wouldn't hesitate to take direct action against him if he interfered, he just wasn't sure what kind of show of force would be appropriate. And he was going to have to give Kyle a call just to get some guidance. He had thought, just like Mia had, that they'd never have to worry about Caesar again.

"Don't worry, sweetheart. We'll figure it out."

THE DINNER WAS delicious, true to its billing. Fredo stuffed himself, and so did the boys. Something that was supposed to be leftover for one or two nights later in the week turned out to be perhaps a snack and not enough for a full meal for any of them. Fredo spoke little, thinking about the situation with Caesar and wondering who from the team he could take with him to go talk to the guy. Maybe he didn't quite have the fight in him that everybody was expecting. Maybe he just wanted to live the rest of his life outside the boundaries of the violence that he had perpetrated. It did happen occasionally, but Fredo didn't expect it.

Ricardo no longer liked to be hugged and kissed by his dad, but he did allow Mia to give him a loving kiss. And at last, all of the boys were in bed.

They came downstairs, and Mia fixed both of them a sangria, adding plenty of orange juice and ginger ale. Fredo was glad that the alcohol level had been tamed.

They sat outside by the pool in lounge chairs, enjoying the warm late spring night and the stars that were starting to poke out from the turquoise sky. All during their time in Mexico, he kept scanning his phone for weather reports of San Diego, and he knew that they'd had a nice mild weather pattern, but mostly with sun. He was so lucky to be living in San Diego. He almost needed to pinch himself.

Finally, he reached out to Mia with one hand. Her

legs were stretched out on her lounge chair, and as she gripped his hand, she turned slightly on her hip so she could study him.

"I think this type of clown is going to have to receive a warning pretty quickly. There's always the possibility it'll make it worse, but if he's changed at all or he's not going to be interested in actually being Ricardo's father in any way, shape, manner, or form, maybe it won't be a problem, Mia."

"I just don't see that. He thinks he owns everything. He thought he owned me, he thought the baby was his, and now Ricardo is a young man. He's going to want Ricardo to follow in his footsteps. And that's the strange thing about this whole thing. He knows this isn't good for him. Ricardo has a good life being a good kid, a good student, and has a brilliant future. You would think if he cared about his son at all that he would just back out and leave us all alone."

"But that's not the way of it, is it?" Fredo asked.

"No. I'm sad to report that I think you're right. So how do we go about approaching him or letting him know we're not afraid of him or of getting the authorities involved so that he would risk going back to prison?"

"Well, we need to find out what the DA is going to do. If he's going to re-arrest him, we want to help him along with that. I don't want to kick the hornet's nest or anything, but when he gets upset, he kind of does just that. That's a good reason to keep him behind bars. On the other hand, if he's learned some kind of self-control over these past nine years, I suppose supervised visits with Ricardo might be in order. But definitely not for a weekend. And we're going to have to work on that. It might be a fight."

"That's exactly what I was thinking. We have a lot of work to do to figure it out, Fredo."

"Do you have any information about what he will be doing if he comes back here?" he asked her.

"Oh, I know what he'll be doing. He's going to run drugs."

"And he's going to try to sell off the kids that he's still holding. The good news about our situation now is that they will have to catch him doing something illegal, and we're going to have to strategize. How's Ricardo holding up about this? He seemed okay to me."

Mia nodded. "He's a good kid, Fredo. You've instilled in him some good values. He's not a hothead. I'm guessing there was a lot more bravado because of who told Ricardo about the release."

Fredo agreed. "They probably built it up to be something way bigger than it is. I'm sure he's going to have to check in daily, maybe wear an ankle monitor, if they still think there's enough evidence to charge him."

"Do you think perhaps you should talk to the warden, ask him some questions about his behavior?"

"I could do that. I just want to be very careful, though. I don't want to worry about something that isn't going to happen. That's the main goal."

Fredo admired his beautiful wife, the only woman in the whole world Fredo could have ever loved, the woman he had to work so hard to woo and who had rejected him over and over again until finally she saw the light, and since then, they'd been one of the happiest couples of all the Team couples. Fredo would be devastated if something ever happened to Mia and, of course, Ricardo as well. He halfway wished he could just pay someone to get rid of him, but that was only a fleeting thought and not anything realistic. It would be certainly something that would cost him his career and possibly several of his friends' careers as well. He couldn't let that happen. And he'd wind up in jail on premeditated murder. Unlike career criminals, Fredo would be locked up, and they'd throw away the key.

"Is he safe at school? I mean, do they have these boys in the same classes?" Fredo asked.

"Yes, I believe the morning class is three days a week, and the afternoon session is twice a week. As you know, the twins are split up."

"So what has Ricardo said about all this. I know he's a good kid, but you'd know. You told me he was acting quiet, upset. Any idea his thoughts?"

"He's okay. He's a really strong kid. But you have to promise me, Fredo, you will not use him as bait to lure Caesar out of some dark hole. I don't want you to put him in harm's way. If we have to, we should move."

Fredo could not come to any conclusions, since he just didn't have enough information. The thought of moving scared him now that they had put down such deep roots in the community. They'd been saving for years for the pool and, last summer, finally had it put in. It kept the boys at home, and they brought their friends, so both Mia and Fredo could check on who they hung with. Not spying, just being strategic, Fredo thought.

First thing he was going to do tomorrow was get some of those answers, and then they could make a decision on which direction to take. It was always about that, assessing the risk and weighing it for the reward. She didn't want direct interaction between him and her ex, but if that was the only way to keep his family safe, he knew he'd do it, even if it cost him his freedom.

As he looked at Mia's beautiful body, all the softness, the peaks, and valleys of her feminine mystique he could never get enough of, his heart expanded and then melted. He was awash with his love for her, every single cell of his body craved her more than he thought possible, and it was growing stronger year by year. He could easily get lost in the aura of her love. He would gladly die to save her and Ricardo. But his real mission was to bring the entire family into safety, including himself.

First thing tomorrow, he was going to need to talk to Kyle.

CHAPTER 6

MIA WOKE UP to the first light of day, initially startled with the panic that perhaps she'd over-slept. Last night had been a wonderful celebration, a welcoming home of the love and support she gave and received from her man. Fredo had always been an attentive lover, never stopping to show her how much he worshiped her body and soul. He never once, even after this almost decade of marriage, dialed that back or got tired of letting her know how important she was to him. It was just something she never expected. And their relationship had bloomed in all aspects of their life. They enjoyed teaching their children, they enjoyed projects together, and they just plain enjoyed everything they did together, including sex.

She smelled bacon cooking, and with the obvious conclusion it had to be Fredo, since his side of the bed was now vacant, she was grateful he had let her sleep, gotten up, and from the sounds of it, gotten the boys up and ready for school. Now she was the recipient of his warm love.

She fell back into the pillow and scanned the ceiling. Fredo had never complained that she didn't bring home a paycheck. He wanted her front and center with the boys, all the way up to doing homeschooling. But since Mia's knowledge of math and English, which had become her second language, was limited and left her feeling inadequate to teach, she resisted the homeschooling. Several of the SEAL wives had begun groups of teaching pods, which interested her, but she was concerned that she wouldn't be able to contribute and since the boys loved St. Cecilia's School, for now this was the logical choice.

Taking a deep breath, her hands shot up above her head on both sides of her ears as she stretched and luxuriated in the few extra moments of sleep Fredo afforded her.

And just at that moment, he walked into the bedroom with a steaming cup of coffee.

"Ah, I see the princess has awakened."

"Thank you, mi amore. It smells great downstairs. I'm assuming the boys are all ready?"

"You've got that right. Got you covered, so why don't you just stay in bed and hold that pose for a while. I'll be back in about a half an hour to forty-five minutes, and maybe we can find something else we can do in this room. Do you suppose this can be done?"

Fredo grinned at her, a lascivious grin only he could make. It was quite obvious Fredo felt they were ready for round two.

"That sounds like a lovely idea. Maybe I should take a shower and put on a new nightie?"

"Why don't you just take a shower and not put on the nightie? I like that too."

"Your wish is my command."

"Oh, don't get me started. I can make a lot of demands on you. You ain't seen nothing yet."

She drew her feet to the floor, stretched, and took another sip of her coffee. "Fredo, I was thinking we should talk to the administrators at St. Cecilia, maybe let them know about this situation with Caesar and his minions? What do you think?"

"I could do it after I drop them off. It's probably something we should schedule and sit down together though. I'd feel better if you were there. Why don't I make an appointment? Then we can kind of sort out and strategize what we're going to say. How about that?"

"Works for me."

Mia took her shower and then gave Christy Lansdowne a call. She thought it would be a good idea if their "team mom" knew about the situation they were facing with Ricardo. She knew that Kyle would want to know and notifying him would be Fredo's job. But it was also important to notify his wife, Christy, and that was her job.

"I'll bet you're glad he's back," said Christy on the phone.

"Always. He even let me sleep in this morning, made breakfast and everything for the boys, and took them to school."

"You know, I knew the very first time I met Fredo that he was just one of those guys who would do anything for his family. Not that Kyle isn't that way as well, but I think the way he demonstrates his love for you, his patience over all those years of angst he had to endure—"

"You mean all the crap I put him through?" interrupted Mia.

"No, it was just something you had to arrive on your own. You decided to change your lifestyle, and I respect that. I think Fredo saw it in you before you did yourself, and if there ever was a couple where marriage enhanced everything about them, you guys would be the poster children for it."

"Wow. Oh my God, Christy. You're making me embarrassed now."

"Okay, I'll stop. So what's up?"

"I'm sure Fredo's going to talk to Kyle about it, but Ricardo had an incident at school the day before yesterday, and Caesar, his biological dad—"

"I know who he is. The cretin who fathered Ricardo?"

"Exactly. Even Ricardo calls him the sperm donor, which I rather like. Anyway, it looks like Caesar has been released from prison, without any notification to our side. I'm not sure why and how this happened, and we're looking into it, but some kids that are younger brothers of gang members and wannabees on the periphery of the Scorpions, sort of intimidated Ricardo and told him that his dad wanted to have a relationship with him or something like that. Anyway, it scared the *cajónes* off my son, and he's upset, as he should be. He's thirteen, he's not a grown man, and he has no interest in having a relationship with his father, who really isn't his father. Fredo is. But he's afraid of this man who supposedly wants to now be part of his life. We haven't verified all of this, but we're just sort of wondering what we should do and looking for advice."

"Oh my God, Mia. This is horrible news. And of course you can't just sweep it under the rug, can you?"

"Hardly. Even my mother is concerned, of course, and Gus as well. I've spoken to him yesterday, and he's about ready to put his belt on and go after the guy I think. Fredo is right to not want to kick the hornet's nest, as he calls it, but we're also concerned that if we don't say something that Caesar will take advantage of that or perceive it as weakness. You know what I mean?"

"Yes. Makes sense. Bullies and bad guys are like that. The good news is when they're like that they're stupid, and they don't think things out. But they have evil minds. You've definitely got my attention. And I'll make sure Kyle hears about it from me. But you're right, Fredo needs to talk to him himself."

"So we're going to contact the school, I think, and then we're going to need a good attorney. Might I ask you if you have any recommendations?"

"Geez, the only attorneys I deal with are real estate attorneys. I'm going to have to ask around. And I just don't know anybody right now who's going through some kind of a custody battle. It's like a family law attorney you need."

"No, we really need a criminal attorney. We need somebody to go after this guy and get him put back behind bars. I don't know how he got off, but it was a poor decision at best, and at worst, somebody got paid off. I would love to be able to find out."

"Well, Mia, let me put some thought into it, and I'll also ask Kyle. Sometimes he knows more about what's going on with some of these families. You know the guys talk. I just don't recall having any of the wives go through this type of thing. We've had divorces and custody battles but not like this, not when someone's come home from prison and wants to insert himself into a family that he nearly destroyed. I just gotta have faith in our justice system, Mia. Why would they allow somebody who almost killed you and your son, why would they allow him to have any kind of access?" Christy asked.

"Money talks. But yes, I agree with you. I'm going to hang my hat on that. Anyway, thanks for picking up. I know you're busy, and I'll let you know if I have any news."

"You do that. Please, Mia, if you need anything at all, if you need a place for the boys to come stay for a while, anything at all, you let me know, and we'll be there for you. Don't worry about that. How did Fredo take the news?"

"Well, we're in the 'let's think about this and strategize' phase. I'm grateful that my husband has matured in his fifteen years as a SEAL. I have a feeling when he first joined, his reaction wouldn't have been like that."

"Oh, yes, they do like to figure things out. Ad nauseum. Not all of them, of course, but it's nice to see that even men of action can mature. And they do that because they have more at stake with wives and kids. They stop doing stupid things."

Mia chuckled, and added, "Except they still jump out of airplanes in the middle of the night at 13,000 feet."

"Touché. Yes, they still do that."

Just as Mia hung up the phone, she heard Fredo's distinctive greet.

"Hello, Lucy, I am home!"

Fredo did a perfect imitation of Desi Arnaz, from the *I Love Lucy* series, which was one of the old TV shows both she and Fredo loved watching.

He tore up the stairs, probably taking two or three at a time, and was in the doorway casually leaning against it, eyeing the sight of her naked body sitting on the bed.

"So this is what I like, a beautiful woman, no clothes, not even a nightie, sitting and waiting for me to come home. I like this, Mia. I like it more every time I see it."

"Well, then why don't you come over here, and I'll show you how excited I am that you're back?"

Fredo made it to the bed in less than a minute, and during the time he was traversing the room in a bunny hop, he was getting rid of his clothes, including his canvas slip-ons.

CHAPTER 7

FREDO WAS IN the shower, getting his first of the day, while Mia soaked off his backside, getting her second. With soap everywhere on both of them, Fredo heard his cell phone ring. He would let it go, except that he had placed a call to Kyle and guessed it could be his return call.

"Oh shit, I think that's Kyle."

"No, no, no! You have to rinse off first, you're not going to be running across our floor with soap down your ass," Mia said.

He quickly turned his back to her, and she used the wand to rinse him off, instructed him to turn to his front side, and repeated the motion. "Now go." She spanked him on the butt cheek as he left the shower, running for his telephone.

"And don't fall!"

"Oh shit, shit, shit," Fredo whispered while he tried to run carefully until he reached his phone.

"Hello, hello, hello, I'm here," Fredo shouted.

"I was just going to hang up. I figured leaving you a message was going to be useless since you never listen to your messages, Fredo. How the hell you doing?"

Kyle's familiar voice barked at him in a pretend dress down.

"Dammit, Kyle we've only been home, what, thirty-five hours?"

"That's a long time to the life of a fruit fly."

"Very funny. I happened to be taking a shower with my lovely wife. So let's make this quick. Otherwise—" He noted Mia wrapped in a towel standing in the doorway to their bathroom. "Oh, crap. It's too late."

"Okay then, Fredo. You'll have to find time for that later. I think it's admirable that you extricated yourself in time to talk to your old LPO. I did listen to my message you left, and I'm concerned. But I'm calling you back to give you the benefit of some information."

"You heard something about Caesar?"

"Yes sir, I did. I also talked to your father-in-law, Gus Mayfield, and he has some connections in the prison system. Turns out, he got himself a judge who isn't going to be up for reelection for another four years, and they've suspected that he's in the pockets of the cartels. They're not pulling any punches anymore. They're not letting anybody get away with not being loyal, so Judge Mathers has granted Caesar a dismissal of all charges and vacated the judgment to time served. You do know he was due to get out in twelve years, not thirty as you told everyone, as we all thought."

"I didn't know that. So he got out three years early then?"

"That's about it. Apparently, he was a model prisoner, and he's convinced a lot of people he's going to turn his life around. I'm not holding my breath for that. His gang still says they hang with him, and well, we know all the crap he pulled. So it's a good cover, but I don't think it's going to fool any of us. Might cause you a problem, though."

"I hate to hear that. So in that situation, can somebody who's served time for endangering a child actually get rights back to have visitations?"

"Well, I'm not an attorney, but I've got a couple names for you. There is such a thing as court-supervised visitation, but you're going to need help with that. And you don't want to be the one paying that bill. It's expensive. I'll text their numbers over in a few. Give them a try—I generally try to stay away from them."

"You got nothing to worry about, Kyle. But I hear you on that one. So do you know anybody who's been through this, like what we're walking into here?"

"Not on the Teams. But hey, I'm sure it's happened a lot. The way things are down here, well, let's just say it's not getting any healthier. Next, they'll be asking us to pack up and ship out to Norfolk or something. It's not going in the right direction. So I want you to be smart, Fredo. Don't go off doing something you know we'll all regret. And I really don't want you dragging any of the guys into this. You hear me on that?"

"Yes, Boss."

"I get that they would probably come and help you, but I just don't need that shit right now. I know you guys would back me up in a firefight if we were overseas, and that's what the brass tries to do—keep us out of trouble—but these types of things, these interpersonal things, husband and wife, even though her ex is a dickwad, we just have to keep our hands out of the cookie jar. So I'm telling you right now, Fredo, don't do that. You stand down."

"And what? Get ready for something to happen before we can go after him?"

"You know I can't give you that kind of advice, Fredo. I don't dare tell you to go get even. At the same time, I know what I'd do in that case. But we have to be smart. There's all kinds of really brilliant people out there a hell of a lot smarter than you and me. Let's use them. And you know if it's money, we'll see if we can set up a fundraiser or something. I know you guys aren't rich. Got all those kids to support, and the attorneys are not cheap. But we'll see if we can find somebody who might be owing us a favor or is just grateful for something we did for them. They're out there too. San Diego has tons of great attorneys."

"As far as schools and all of that, Ricardo runs into these guys at school, and of course, the twins also go to St. Cecilia's. Should we consider transferring them? You certainly wouldn't recommend going into public school, would you?"

"Oh, I think public school would be worse, don't you?"

"Yeah, you're right. But these kids start causing a problem at the school and administration is apt to use the hatchet approach."

"Now that sounds like something we do. I can't see a bunch of nuns running around with hatchets."

Fredo chuckled. "You'd be surprised what they do. But no, not real hatchets. What I mean to say is they kick everybody out. Unlike school districts where they have to give warnings and counsel the parents and try to come to a peaceful resolution, the sisters don't mess around with this stuff. They run a very tight ship. Even though he's the one being picked on, they're just as likely to ask him to leave the school too. They hate press, and they hate other parents reading that there is some kind of gang violence at school."

"I can see that," Kyle said. "No controversy. Sweep it under the rug sort of thing."

That gave Fredo an idea. "So what if the kids got arrested or, you know, ran into trouble with the law somehow? What if it's not like a big fight involving Ricardo? Then they'd kind of be forced to do something, right? I mean, I don't wish them any ill will. Shoot, they're still preteens, for Christ's sake. They're not smart enough to realize if they just keep their heads cool it would work out better for them. But they don't have that maturity. If we could get these kids written up or get their names in the paper somehow, it would be easy to also request that they be released and say that Ricardo had been hassled by them."

"Well, that's a thought. Personally, I'd stay away from that as if my life depended on it. They don't like to be messed with, Fredo. If you're going to go with that approach, then you probably ought to keep all this a secret. You want the papers to tell them. You don't say a word about it."

"But if I don't warn them at the school, Caesar might show up and claim he's the boy's father and take him. Or strong-arm take him. I doubt they'd willingly let him go."

"That's right, Fredo. They'll stand up to him until it crosses a certain threshold, and then they don't want to have violence, so they'll cave, and I think Caesar's cohorts know that too. But maybe that's the way to go. You and Mia talk about it. I'm sure you're going to come up with the right decision. Your biggest problem now is going to be raising the money just in case you need one of those high-powered attorneys I'm going to get you. Oh, and by the way, thanks for the compliment."

"What?"

"Well, Christy said Mia told her that you were leading the charge to sit down and reasonably strategize and do a risk-reward type scenario. And she said you told her that it came from me. So thank you."

"You're welcome." But Fredo knew those words were never said. Christy was just buttering him up to make the phone call.

"So how's the kid?" Fredo asked.

"I was going to go run by there in a few minutes. Are you dressed yet or not finished in the bedroom?"

"Fuck you. I could have my share of the fun. I got married a lot later than you did, so get off my case. You know it's kind of ironic, I thought I'd never have any kids, except for Ricardo. But before Mia and I solidly decided to get married, and it was a real commitment not just a dating situation, I thought I'd never have kids of my own, and now I've got three. And now I'm even thinking about maybe adding a fourth."

Kyle sighed in exasperation. "So I'm going to guess, Fredo, you didn't tell Mia yet about the kid, right?"

"That's correct. We had this other thing to talk

about."

"And that's important, it really is. But here's the thing, Fredo. She's the one that's got to do the work, so she's the one that's got to choose. I don't see how you can even put your hat in the ring until this thing with Ricardo is taken care of. And let's be honest with each other, Fredo. How would you feel if you were a ten-year-old kid coming into a strange family, not knowing how to properly speak English, new country, new people, new schools, new cultures. How would you feel if there was a whole lot of drama about some asshole drug dealer hassling your new mom and your new stepbrother? Don't you think he'd feel a little uneasy. Maybe a tad bit uncomfortable?"

Fredo thought Kyle made tremendous sense, but something in his gut still told him that this little boy who stood up to forces much greater than himself, this little boy deserved a chance, just like Ricardo had needed a father to step in and assume the duties that his biological father would never do. Fredo always considered himself someone who saved the innocent, and that's what he intended to do.

But there was Mia. And if she said no, it would be no. He was sure someone else would step up. He thought about going over to the hospital with Kyle and decided to jump in.

"Okay, Kyle, I'm on board. You can pick me up in

just a few minutes. At least I'm showered. I might still have some soap on me, but I'm clean. I'll be ready when you get here."

THE HOSPITAL WAS busy today, even the main lobby was filled with people waiting. The hospital also had a physical therapy wing and prosthetic services for veterans. They were locally known as one of the best in Southern California.

"Geez, Kyle, if this is how busy the main lobby is, the ER room must be a zoo," said Fredo.

"I think you're right."

They inquired at the reception desk first of all to make sure the kid was still registered, and he was, and second to see if he was being allowed friends and next of kin.

The woman behind the desk pushed her thick, round, bright-red glasses back onto her nose. "You are relatives?" she said in a thick Latin accent.

"We are not, except we helped rescue him. We just want to check on him is all. We won't stay long. Can you check your notes and see if he's conscious?" Kyle poured on the sweetness as only he could do. Fredo had seen it hundreds of times.

"I see here that there are restrictions on his visitors. I will not be able to give you his status. But if you wait, I'll let you speak to his attending physician, who's still here from morning rounds. I'm sure he'd be glad to talk to you properly. I'm really not supposed to give out any information."

Fredo leaned forward and practically barked at the woman. "But he's still alive, right?"

"Sí, señor. He is alive. I think the doctor will be able to give you a much better idea of what his current condition is, so I will have him paged."

They sat on a round donut-shaped leather cushion with a hole in the middle. It did resemble a glazed donut, no question about it. Fredo was suddenly hungry for something sweet.

"You want to get a coffee, or you want me to get some?" Fredo asked.

"Sure. I'm going to wait here for the doc, but I'll text you if he shows up. You go grab something for yourself. If they've got bagels and cream cheese, I'll take it."

"Anything else? Coffee?" Fredo asked.

"No, I'm good. I got my water."

Walking down the hallway, it was common to hear multiple languages spoken, as several immigrant families used the hospital's emergency room for routine office care. He heard dialects from all over Central and South America, several he'd never heard before.

He hoped there was some improvement today, and

he was looking forward to being able to question the kid about some of the things he had seen. He purchased a bagel with everything on it for Kyle and one smothered in cream cheese for himself, along with a coffee and cream. When he got back to the lobby, the doctor was speaking with Kyle.

Fredo handed Kyle his bagel.

"Perfect. Now my stomach will stop rumbling. So, Fredo, this is Dr. Halprin. He's one of the best surgeons down here, I think you remember him from yesterday morning?"

"Sure do." He extended his hand and shook the doctor's.

"Good to see you again. You guys did a hell of a job," Dr. Halprin said.

"Thanks for taking good care of Ivan. Do you have good news for us?" Fredo asked.

"Yeah, I was just telling your LPO here, he's making very good improvement. Of course, it's still too early to tell. He suffered quite a bit, the loss of blood is something that sometimes winds up being problematic later on, but even though he is skinny, he's healthy. Somebody's been feeding him."

"So he's eating then?" Fredo asked.

"Just a few bites here and there, not a lot, and that's normal. In time, after his surgeries, we're going to have to take a look at him and do some tests, but as of right now, I'd say he's well on his way to recovery. And he'll be a lot more comfortable if I can get him off the pain meds and get him something that won't be so devastating to him."

"You mean he's awake?" Fredo asked.

"Yes, he woke up early this morning. Well, he was in pain. He was having a hard time sleeping because of the pain, and he made us promise that he'd have no visitors. I wasn't planning on anything, but then when they told me last night after I went home that he woke up, I figured I'd better get down here first thing this morning and do some evaluations. I was about to go in. Do you want to come in with?"

"Hallelujah," Kyle said.

"Oh, the both of you?" The doctor looked puzzled for a few seconds. Then he continued. "Oh, what the hell, I'll have you both go in. Kyle, let me get you a lab coat, okay?"

"Fine by me."

The boy's face was swollen such that he would be difficult for Fredo to recognize if it weren't for the setting and the fact that he was familiar with his injuries. His head was bandaged above his eyebrows, and he had a cast on his right arm, but it was his left arm that had really suffered the brunt of the kicking and treatment he'd gotten at the hands of the guards. His eyes opened and closed softly. His focusing abilities took some time to kick in, but when he looked back and forth between Fredo and Kyle, he came up with a weak-looking grin. In Spanish, he said, "My saviors."

The doctor looked at Fredo, asking for a translation.

"He called us his saviors. That's nice." In Spanish, Fredo responded. "You're a tough kid, and I'm so sorry for what you have been through. We, all three of us," And motioned to the doctor, Kyle, and himself, "we're here to help make it so that you never have to experience that again." He paused, just to see if the boy had recognition of what he was talking about.

"Where am I?" the boy asked in Spanish.

Fredo translated the answer. "You're in the USA. San Diego. Scripps Hospital. I go here sometimes," Fredo said. "This here is your doctor, and he is one of the best surgeons in this whole area. You were lucky he was on call and here in the emergency room when they brought you in. He's going to try to make it so that you experience less pain, but he has told us that he can't do that until he does perhaps another surgery. But I will translate for him so he can tell you himself."

Ivan nodded his head, fully understanding.

"I am grateful you brought me here."

"We'd like to come back and talk to you about your trip," Kyle started, "But we don't want to tire you.

Perhaps we could see you tomorrow? Is that okay?"

Fredo translated. "Sí, I would like that very much."

Kyle then asked if he needed anything.

The boy answered in Spanish, but everyone standing around the bed knew what he wanted.

"I need my mother and my little sister."

CHAPTER 8

WHILE FREDO WAS off with Kyle, Mia picked the boys up from school. Today, Ricardo wasn't talkative at all, and she tried to pry out of him if any additional hassling had been done by the boys. She soon realized her prying was not getting any results.

Ricardo's math teacher was a friend of Mia's, had dated a former SEAL for a period of time but still was single after the death of her first husband. She wondered if perhaps Adrienne could shed some light on how Ricardo was doing. She decided she would schedule a parent-teacher conference. But she wouldn't share what was going on with Ricardo's biological father.

"So no further incidents then, is that what you're saying?"

"Oh, I wouldn't say that. They glared at me. But those assholes, I think they glare at everybody. Maybe I blew it too much out of proportion, Mom. I'm just going to forget about all that shit."

"Ricardo!"

"I'm sorry. It's just sort of annoying, and I let it slip. I really am sorry, Mom. I don't do that very much."

"Well, I don't want you to do it at all, especially in front of your younger brothers."

"Well, they're going to learn it if they don't already know. You can't keep them as babies forever. They got to grow up. And they'll find out, the world's kind of a nasty place sometimes."

Mia wondered where all this modern introspection came from. It was hard to say what was influencing Ricardo these days. He'd been placed in an advanced reading class and was flying through the books he was given. The teacher told Mia he was the best student in the class. Yet, Ricardo never talked about those books or how come the love of reading had just taken off this year. Whatever was the reason for it, Mia was glad.

"How about this, then? If we decide to take a family vacation this year, and again it all depends on what your dad's schedule is, is there any place in particular you'd like to go?"

From the backseat came the unanimous shout-out, "Disney World!"

"I asked Ricardo. We'll get there. I don't want to spend that kind of money just yet." And then to

Ricardo in a lower tone, she said, "Would you like to do something just you and your dad? You could go skydiving maybe or he could take you out shooting. Some of the guys go hunting. Does that interest you at all?"

"Sure, I love all those things, but guns? They make me nervous."

Mia knew what Fredo would say if he was here. She tried to paraphrase it as best she could.

"Well, that's probably because you haven't had enough training using guns. But it's not something you have to do. You wouldn't be expected to defend your family. It'll be another story after you leave the house, go off, and get married."

"Who said anything about marriage? I'm thirteen, Mom. I don't ever think about that one."

Mia quickly glanced over at her son, saw the expression on his face, and understood the addiction to girls had not yet begun. Perhaps it was better that Ricardo was a little bit of a late bloomer. God knows, Mia wasn't that way at all. And she'd driven her mother crazy. She should be grateful.

"Well, you think about it. It's got to be your idea, and if we can swing it, if it's something not all five of us can do but just you and your dad or the three of us, if it's within reason and not too expensive, we'll do it."

Ricardo stared at her. "Are you buttering me up so

you can drop the hammer on me later? What is it you really want, Mom?"

"I just want you to feel like you can tell me anything. I want you to understand that we have your back. I know it's probably confusing, and a big part of it's my fault for having made certain choices perhaps I shouldn't have. But if I hadn't, you wouldn't be here today. So I guess good can come from bad. I'm just hoping we don't have to see Caesar very much in the future. We're working on that anyway."

"I don't understand why he wants to have anything to do with me. I'm not anything like him, from the stories I've heard anyway. I don't want to be a wannabe 'gangsta.' I don't want to be hanging around the shopping centers and cemeteries and parks at night, I don't want to get in trouble. That's just dumb."

"I'm glad you see it that way, Ricardo. That's healthy. I wish everybody had that kind of maturity."

"I think some of the guys at school who brag about some of the things they've done, they are trying to fool themselves into thinking they're big badass dudes."

"Ricardo, I don't like that tone of voice, and I don't like you swearing. What's gotten into you?"

"Nothing, I'm just like I always was."

Mia decided it was time to stop pestering him with questions, since it was obvious her probing was not getting her very far, and she needed all the connection with him she could get. If things got really heated, he didn't need to have both sides of his family turn into a nightmare. She wanted to remain close to him.

"You know I love you, right?"

"Yeah, I do. I think you and Dad have done a great job. You both work hard. I'm proud of our family. Some guys at school, their sisters or their cousins or sometimes their mothers, they embarrass them. I don't feel that way about you guys. And most people when they find out what Dad does, well, they're in awe. I mean, not everybody can do the kind of stuff he does."

"I'm glad you see it that way, Ricardo. Your dad's a very special man. Not everybody is physically capable and emotionally capable of doing some of the ops that he completes. He doesn't talk about it much because he doesn't do it for fame and glory or recognition of any kind. He does it because it's his calling, because he doesn't want to see innocent people get preyed on by cretins. So we're charged with keeping the faith, keeping the home fires burning, and making sure Fredo knows that we appreciate him. I think he'd rather have your respect than anything else in the world. I know he loves you, but even more important, he values you."

When they got to the house, the twins were sent upstairs to begin their homework while Ricardo was given the dining room table to work on his. He had a computer upstairs in his bedroom but the computer the whole family used downstairs was connected to the printer and Ricardo wanted to be able to make notes and print them out so he wouldn't forget the references.

"I know you've got a report for history. How's it coming?" Mia asked Ricardo.

"It's coming. I'm going to finish it this weekend, but that's why I got the book so I can work on it, because I have to turn it in on Friday. I can't keep it over the weekend."

"Good job, Ricardo. How did you pick the mission in Santa Clara to do your study on?"

"Remember last summer when I went up to play soccer at that tournament in Santa Clara?"

"Yes, Fredo took you. I don't think I went to that one, but gosh, I've been to so many."

"No, Mom, you didn't go to that one. Anyway we got to know the kids on the local United team. They were fourteen-year-olds kind of all puffed out and feeling superior, and then when we beat them, we came in second place in the whole tournament. Well, since we obviously were impressing people with the size and the quickness of our team, they started being nice to us and showed us around. One guy took several of us on a tour of the chapel at Santa Clara. Did you know, Mom, that they have Indians buried in the walls?"

Mia scrunched up her nose. "I'm not so sure about that. We call them Native Americans now. But they told you that?"

"Yes, they said some of the priests that were there, the fathers, and some of the elders from the village were buried within the walls because it took a couple of years to finish the whole mission complex. Anyway it gave me an excuse to go look up that theory, and I haven't verified it, but it's kind of an interesting issue."

"I could see how that would capture your attention. I'd take it with a grain of salt, Ricardo. I never heard that growing up, but then we didn't live on the Peninsula either. We lived for the first many years of my life in Puerto Rico. And trust me, they didn't put Indians' bodies into the concrete there."

"Well, we all thought it was kind of cool. Somebody said that when the organ gets played late at night, there's spirits that come from the ground up, singing. It's kind of creepy if you ask me. But I got enough material for a good report without having to bring up all of that. But you asked me why, so I just told you."

"Well, whatever reason you have to do a study of the mission at Santa Clara, I completely approve. As long as we don't have ghosts flying around, ghost stories, cattle mutilations, all that stuff. And who knows, maybe it was a wives' tale told just to keep people out of the church. I think it would scare me."

"Well, it does scare me. I think about it all the time. We'll have to go there sometime. I think you'd like the history of it."

"You know, we could do a long weekend sometime, come up and do that road trip. I'm afraid it's out of the cards before your paper's due, but I think you've obviously got a lot of questions, and maybe the sisters will put you in contact with a researcher there. There's a famous University there."

Just then, they heard screaming upstairs in the boys' bedroom. Mia banged on the door.

"Open up, this is your mother speaking. I want no more of that roughhousing going on."

She came back downstairs and started to load up the dishwasher, tidying the kitchen. She needed a few things at the store for dinner but didn't want to leave all the boys together without an adult. But then she heard Fredo's Hummer park in their driveway.

She brushed her hair, fluffed it out—long and wild was how he liked it—and then greeted him at the doorway.

"Well, Sailor. Are you going to be here long?"

"I think so. I'm sticking around your whole life, sweetheart. Trust me on that." He walked right past her into the living room and on to the kitchen. His routine, without the warmth.

But he usually smiled after that or gave her a hug, a

kiss, or something tender. Even the boys couldn't elicit a wrestle or some high fives. It wasn't his lack of interest. It was something else.

Fredo was in one of those moods where she couldn't tell whether he was on solid ground or not. The boys greeted their dad when he entered the kitchen, dropping his duffel bag unceremoniously right by the kitchen rear doorway. It had been their tradition. Fredo was to give up his dirty clothes. This time he was late, but that had happened before, so Mia knew they'd be extra ripe sitting in the hot sun of the Hummer's interior. Then Mia would set upon getting everything cleaned and folded to his specifications, ready for his next deployment.

But today, he was distracted and didn't seem to hear anything Mia had said.

The boys finished their afterschool snack and headed for the pool. Every time she saw them jump in, every time she wrote that monthly check, she was grateful they'd splurged for the pool, even though they could not really afford it on Fredo's military salary. It was an investment in their happiness.

But not even the blue-turquoise pool could entice Fredo into a more playful demeanor. She decided to keep trying, but be very careful about it. Never push. Keep the criticism logical and with provable facts and details. Only things emotional Fredo liked was their lovemaking, and then she could come off the rails, and he'd be in the best mood ever. Funny how that worked. If she could show him how much pleasure he brought her, if he could feel it in the beating of her heart and her breathless pants after the exhaustive sexual encounter, he'd believe it. But just telling him or asking questions wasn't the way.

It wasn't really play-acting, although some might think so. It was fulfilling the role she'd chosen, why he'd chosen her, because she wanted to be all the things he wanted and limit the things he didn't. Far from submission, working hard to understand and be the best wife any SEAL could have had become her joy. He deserved it, and she did to. It worked both ways for them both.

Right now was going to be the heavy lifting time. Done with grace and showing her caring side, not her angry or critical side.

Showtime!

"You've been out in the sun. Go take a shower, and I'll get these started in the wash."

He nodded to the floor.

"Any snakes, scorpions? Any dead furry animals like last time?"

"Probably should have checked. Why don't you let me load the washer and I'll dispose of anything I find?"

She raised her eyebrows. "I'm a big girl. I've done

this before a time or two. I was just making fun, but I guess my delivery and timing needs work."

That got his attention, and she could see him melt, realizing how he was coming across.

"God, Mia. I've been a fool." He stepped in front of her and grabbed her into his arms. "I was distracted. Forgive me?"

"As long as that distraction isn't a she, blonde, and with a bigger bust than mine."

"No worries there, Mia. No one could ever be anything but a cheap imitation not even worthy of my gaze. I look, but when I see something attractive it does nothing to diminish the joy and love I have with you. You are irreplaceable, one of a kind, and I don't begin to deserve you. I'm glad you listened to my poor pleas, took pity on me, and made me the happy man I am today."

The words were so beautiful, Mia's tears poured out. When Fredo heard her sniffle, he drew back, studying her face before placing a tender kiss on her lips.

"Mi amore," she whispered into his hungry mouth.

He rocked her back and forth, steadying her in his massive arms, rubbing her back up and down her spine with his calloused hands. His battle scars and all.

"The wash can wait. Let's talk," he said.

She brought two glasses of ice water to the table in

the kitchen, where they both sat.

"Was this a difficult morning, Fredo? Something going on with Kyle?"

She remembered too late she was trying not to ask too many questions and silently cursed herself.

"No, that part's fine. I didn't tell you what we found in Mexico. I can't tell you the details just yet until after our debriefing, but we rescued a little migrant boy who had been injured by the men who were trafficking him and his family. We were able to medically evacuate him to Scripps, just in time. He's still very ill, but this morning, he was talking."

"So you went with Kyle to visit him, then," Mia said, suddenly understanding Fredo's mood.

"We did."

Fredo looked at the ice water, the drips of condensation traveling like tears down the glass, then continued. "He's all alone."

"But you said he had family."

"They didn't make it."

"That's terrible. Poor thing. Well, I'm glad you came to give him moral support. Good on you guys for doing that."

But that didn't move Fredo.

"What? What's going on?"

"The timing sucks, but I was going to ask you if we could apply to adopt him."

"We don't know him, Fredo. You just met, right?"

"Sometimes you know things about people instantly. Things like bravery, courage, how it feels to lose a parent, or, in his case, I think both his parents and a sibling. His whole world. He's going to be needing lots of medical help and his recovery will be long. But that little boy is a warrior, and he stood up to pure evil like few grown men do today. I think watching that had the same effect on the whole platoon. I even saw some tears on guys I've never seen cry before, Mia. Bravery comes in all sizes, colors, all nationalities, but once you witness it, you are forever changed."

Mia touched his hand, and he squeezed her fingers.

"Of course, it would change you. I wouldn't expect anything less," she whispered.

"It's the part of my job that I love because it masks some of the evil parts of my job. I'm not sure I'm suited to do anything else. But I do think I've never seen such a strong character in a child. I don't want that wasted, watered down, disregarded, or malnourished. He's all alone in this world. I don't know whether it's for me or for him, but I'd like to try to give a hand-up. And before you ask, it doesn't diminish my love for the boys, either. Or you," he said while squeezing her fingers.

"I understand, Fredo. If you are sure, I'll trust your judgment on this. May I ask that I get to talk to him first before the final decision is made?"

"Ah, Sweetheart," Fredo said as he knelt in front of her, his arms wrapped around her torso. "That is why I love you so much."

A few minutes later, as Fredo was trying to arrange a visit at the hospital for as soon as possible, his cell rang. He hung up and answered it.

"Mr. Chavez?" It was an older woman's voice.

"Yes, ma'am. That's me."

"This is Sister Mary Margaret from St. Cecilia's. You asked to make an appointment with me, and I have some dates and times I thought I'd go over with you. I do have some time this afternoon, if that works. About four? Or tomorrow at noon. And then there's—"

Fredo interrupted her. "How about tomorrow at noon? The boys will be in class, and we'll not have to hire a sitter."

"Very well. I'll put you down. Now, will both you and your wife be coming, or just you?"

He looked into Mia's eyes. She was nodding.

"She'll be with me."

"Good. And I understand you didn't want to reveal your reason for this appointment. Is there some problem here at school concerning one of your boys?"

"They love the school there. This has to do with some family dynamics going on, or what might be going on. We wanted to discuss it with you first in private, see if you had any recommendations for us."

"Of what nature, Mr. Chavez?"

"I think it's best we talk tomorrow. Thank you for being so available."

After Fredo hung up, Mia commented on something she'd noticed.

"You're serious about all this, aren't you? You left the afternoon open so I could possibly visit the boy, right?"

"I did. Still waiting for permission. Can you arrange a sitter?"

Mia looked out at their yard and the water fight ensuing. It was going to be hard to take them out of the pool.

"Let me get the youngest Bennet girl to come over. I know she's saving for college. She might enjoy a dip in the pool herself."

CHAPTER 9

FREDO TOOK MIA'S hand, and they walked down the corridors of the huge hospital complex to Ivan's room. Before they could enter, the head nurse ran over and blocked their entrance.

"You can't go in there without permission. Are you family?" she asked Fredo and then briefly nodded to Mia.

"I'm the fellow that rescued him from Mexico. We are considering filing papers of adoption, and I would like to introduce him to my wife. If he's well enough today. Is he?"

"Well, those aren't reasons that I can give approval. You're going to have to check with his doctor, and he's not here right now, so I'll try to get him on the phone, unless you have his number."

"I have his number. He gave me his card." Fredo pulled it out of his jacket pocket.

"Very well, I will trust you, but please reach him

before you enter the room. And just for your information, he's eating like a horse."

Her once frosty appearance warmed quickly.

Fredo whispered in Mia's ear, "They have special
rules about foreign patients coming in under an
emergency situation. Many of the people who they get
are not immunized for all kinds of diseases that we've
eradicated decades ago. They have to be very careful.
I'm surprised they don't have a sign on the room, so I'll
have to ask about that. And so far there's no DHS
guard, which is also unusual."

With Mia nodding, Fredo heard his line pick up on
the doctor's end.

"Hello? This is Dr. Halprin."

"Hey Doc, it's Fredo Chavez. We met this morning
and yesterday."

"Yes, Fredo, what can I do for you?"

"Your station nurse said I needed your permission
to come see him. My wife wants to meet him since we
are considering that paperwork that we discussed this
morning. Would you be so kind as to allow her to
visit?"

"You're at the hospital now?"

"Yes, sir. I went home, and we got to talking. She
has not met him, and I think it's only fair that she get a
chance to introduce herself. Also, I have some questions I need to ask him about the organization that he

witnessed, and she can be my witness, if you'll allow maybe fifteen, twenty minutes of questioning. If we see he's in any kind of distress, we would gladly leave. But I need your okay on that if you're in agreement."

Dr. Halprin hesitated but then gave his approval. "I don't want to tax his energy, but we do not know everything about his system yet, and if something should pop up and it becomes an emergency situation, I'd rather have given you guys the chance to ask him your important questions. So I'll allow it, but under no circumstances, Mr. Chavez, are you to stay there longer than an hour. And I'm going to tell that to the nurse too. In fact, I'm going to have her monitor his stage of awareness and pain level, and if it agitates him at all, I get all his vitals sent to me directly, I'll be able to see it, and I will cut it off there. So please don't push. It's what's good for him."

"Thanks, Doc. I'm handing the phone over to your nurse here."

After giving the nurse his cell phone, Fredo pointed with his thumb to the door, which was closed, and he and Mia entered the darkened room.

At first, Fredo thought the young boy was sleeping, but then he noticed the front of his face was wet, and he'd been crying. He felt sad and a little guilty about witnessing the fact that he missed his mother and little sister. Perhaps they had pushed their luck too far, and

Fredo certainly didn't want to cause him any more undue stress. But he theorized that the more Ivan learned about Fredo and his Team guys, the more he would like them and the more comfortable he would feel around them. He could only begin to guess what kind of crazy stories these people were being told by the cartels and also by the police in Mexico proper.

"Ivan? It's me, Fredo. Are you open to having a visitor or two?"

Ivan scooched up on the bed, bringing himself to sitting position with his legs extended out front. He did look like the pictures of children's books of *The Princess and the Pea*, where the princess was so tiny compared to the size of the bed with all those mattresses piled up to the ceiling. Ivan had a surgical bed that had more than twenty adjustments and positions to accommodate any kind of surgery, and it was also wide with side panels that pulled down or up or turned into rails, if need be. Ivan leaned forward and gave an inquisitive look at Mia.

Fredo wrapped his arm around his wife and pulled her slowly and gently over to Ivan's bedside. "This is Mia, my wife."

She extended her hand, and little Ivan timidly took the tip of her fingers and shook up and down. In Spanish, he said, "Nice to meet you."

Mia responded in Spanish that she was likewise

charmed. Then she added, "I understand you were quite the little fighter. My husband is very impressed with your bravery. I am so sorry for your loss, and I wish you to know that this gentleman here, my husband, is one of the finest and bravest men I have ever met. Please don't hesitate to remain friends with him. He wants to help you. And you can trust him."

Fredo added, "One of the things you're going to need to do right away is to begin to learn English. That will help you get around much better, will help you find things, and you'll be able to be more involved in your own care if you do that."

Ivan nodded his head. "I am grateful, Señor. I have made some very good first friends. How long do you think I have to stay here?"

Fredo answered him back in Spanish as well. "As I think the doctor told you this morning, he has an additional surgery or two on your shoulder to repair some of the things he couldn't do the first time he went in. I'm going to guess that you'll be here for a few days anyway."

Mia touched Fredo on his shoulder, leaning toward the boy.

"Is there someone that you know that you would like us to contact for you, Ivan? May I call you Ivan?" she asked.

Ivan shook his head from side to side and then

some kind of remembrance crossed his face because his eyes got big, and he looked to the right and the left on the floor for something.

"What is it? Are you looking for your bag?" Fredo asked him.

"Sí. I have it in my bag."

Fredo got down on his knees and searched under the bed and came up empty-handed, but Mia pointed to a closet door directly opposite Ivan's bed. When Fredo opened it, he saw the satchel that Ivan's mother had been wearing when she was shot. There was still blood on it that had not been removed. He tried to ignore it and brought it over carefully to Ivan, turning it around so he might miss the stain. But he didn't. A single tear ran down his left cheek as he zippered the top and rummaged through articles of clothing and some paperwork, one by one laying the things out on his legs when he thought they were important.

"May I?" Mia asked.

Ivan pushed the satchel in her direction. Mia rummaged through the paperwork that Ivan had been disinterested in, placing them all to her right, and searched for other paperwork to add to it. Finally, at the very bottom, something that surprised both of them, was a military dog tag. When Mia held it up, the little silver beads of the necklace hanging down touching the covers on the bed, Ivan perked up and pointed to it.

"This, this. This is my father. My father is in the US. He lives here. My mother was trying to go meet him."

Fredo was distressed with his information. It changed the trajectory of everything they'd been planning. If Ivan had a blood relative who was a US citizen, he would more than likely only be sent to that person. And unless the person was deceased or refused him, only then would there be some kind of an adoption recommended. He decided not to explain this to Ivan, or Mia, until he had time to properly lay it out and get answers.

"So where does your father live then? Where in the US, what state?"

Ivan shook his head and shrugged, holding his hands in front of him, indicating he had no clue.

"I think he doesn't know what a state is," Mia whispered in English.

"You have different regions in Mexico. In the US, it is the same thing. We have states like small countries making up the big United States, which is our US country. It would help me to find your father if you knew where he lived. And from the looks of this dog tag, it appears to be not new. It also appears that your father was a US Marine, is that correct?"

"Sí, sí. Yes, my father is a Marine. I never met him.

I was only a baby when he went back home. My mother was his girlfriend for a period of time. She was a professional girlfriend. You have that in the US?"

Fredo shared a look with Mia.

"Ivan, it's probably also something that women do in the US. However, it may be more prevalent in Mexico. So your father was on vacation, is that what you're saying? What did your mother tell you?"

"She says he made her his wife while he was in Mexico. His Mexican wife. My mother thought that perhaps he had an American wife as well."

"And you don't think he even knows that you exist, is that correct?" Fredo asked.

Ivan looked down at the bag, his lower lip protruded slightly, looking sad and unsure what to say. After a few seconds, he shook his head from side to side. "No."

"Do you have anything else that tells where your father's house is?" asked Mia.

Ivan shrugged again. "Maybe the papers, but I do not read English. There are some papers there in English, I think. My mother paid much money to come here. It was required that it be US dollars. $8,000. That is more money than she made all year working as a housekeeper for a wealthy gentleman. I was surprised that she was able to find the money. And then it was stolen."

"We are going to look through this paperwork, and

do I have your permission to make a copy of some of these things so we can help you find your dad?"

Ivan nodded his approval.

Fredo did manage to find Ivan's certificate of live birth, and on the certificate received from the doctor who delivered him, a form that the doctor filled in blanks, it did list the Marine as being Ivan's father.

That was certainly something he needed to get a copy of, and he also found a letter. It came from California somewhere, but the postmark was smudged. Without a return address, it really was no help. He took out the letter and saw that it was handwritten.

"Would you like me to read this letter? It is, I believe, from your father to your mother. Has she read this to you?"

"I don't think she read it. She does not read English. One of her younger sisters teaches in the school, and she was not able to read it either. So I have never heard it before. Can you read this letter to me so I can hear the voice of my father?"

Fredo stiffened and cleared his throat about to begin the reading, all the while feeling Mia's tense body standing next to him.

"May we sit down?" he asked the boy.

"Sí, sí," and Ivan pointed to the chairs.

"My dear Lupe,

First, I want to tell you how much you mean to

me and how special our month was together while I was visiting Cabo San Lucas. I didn't expect to fall in love, but I did. Now that I am home, unfortunately, the reality of my fun time in Mexico has made me a very sad man. I was not completely honest with you, and I should not have taken advantage of your generosity when you offered to cook and keep house for me. But I will always cherish our April together, and although I probably will never see you again, I hope and pray that you find a wonderful man to make your husband, and I hope that you have a happy and successful life.

I was engaged to be married when I came down to Mexico on that fishing trip. My buddies had been coming down there for years, and they were the ones who said that I should find a girlfriend, a wife for a month. My wife here, as we got married soon after I returned, will never know about you, but I think she would have liked you. I just wanted you to know that because I developed feelings for you, I stepped over the line and took what was offered without taking the responsibility of knowing I had no right to ask that of you. Nor that did I have the right to break the promises I had made to my fiancée, Mary.

But I will always cherish the sunsets, the wonderful fresh fish dishes that you cooked, the homemade tortillas and tamales, and that amazing white pepper sauce that burned the whole inside of my mouth and throat the first time I ate it, but which soon became my staple, and I have yet to find it in any restaurant here.

I am leaving the military and going to work for a farming concern here in California. My father-in-law has a large ranch, and he raises cattle, as well as apples, prunes, peaches, and sometimes other fruits. I have always liked farming, and I was fortunate enough to not be born on a farm, so this, even though it's a lot of work, is fun for me. I think if I had been raised on a farm, it wouldn't be so special.

Please say hello to Adela, to Maria, and Bernadette. I hope you'll remain friends, and I hope all of you find wonderful husbands. I will think of you always, and I think you will always claim a piece of my heart.

Much love, and God bless you,
Lance."

After reading the letter to Ivan, Fredo didn't have the stomach to stay longer and ask him questions about his life in Mexico or the long difficult trek his little family made at great cost. He wanted this to be the last thing Ivan heard before he went to sleep tonight.

There would be more times in the hours to come where they could discuss the nasty business of the smugglers and the heartache and ruin they were spewing everywhere.

He couldn't save Ivan's mother or sister. But he and Mia could give him a little bit of peace, and if it wasn't in the cards to have him come live with them, he could at least help him solve the riddle of finding a forever home he would feel safe in.

He placed his big, calloused hand on the boy's head.

"Goodnight, Son."

He handed back the letter and noticed Ivan pressed it to his chest and held it firm like it was a lifeline.

CHAPTER 10

MIA TEXTED THE babysitter, letting her know that they were on their way home. She asked if the sitter could stay an extra forty-five minutes so she and Fredo could stop and grab something to eat and pick up some pizza for the kids.

The Bennet girl agreed to it enthusiastically and said she was having a great time swimming with the kids in the pool.

Homework was going to have to wait, Mia realized. Tonight, they were just being kids.

Fredo took her to an Italian restaurant, and they ordered an early dinner light fare, selecting a table in a dark corner so they could have some privacy while they talked. They put in their order for the take-out for later, and it was promised to be brought piping hot.

"Fredo, did you have any idea any of this happened in the past? Did he mention it before?" asked Mia.

"Well, before, he was out cold. He was in pretty bad

shape. And at the hospital, he didn't say anything about that, so I'm not sure what to think. I want to believe him, though, and I think with these documents, I'll start looking into it."

Mia noticed Fredo was not smiling, and she suspected all this new information threw him for a loop. He didn't do unexpected consequences well, she knew from nearly ten years of marriage now. But, in these cases, there were probably a thousand different scenarios of the same situation with other crossings at the border every single week.

"The one thing I was struck with, Fredo, is it sounds like he really loved her, but he didn't want to bring her to the States. Because he was already engaged. So first of all, he's kind of a lowlife for doing that to her. And second, I mean, if the guy was super responsible, he would've checked back with her. I'm sure he knew whether or not they'd used protection. So that's kind of irresponsible of him. I don't think I like that."

"No, I didn't like that either, but, who knows, maybe he was just really young." Fredo gave her a sly grin. "I mean, I don't know anybody who made some dumb decisions at eighteen or nineteen years old, do you?"

She smiled. "Oh, I have one little lady in mind. And yes, I know her quite well." She grinned.

"I'm going to check with Gus and see if he knows

how we can quickly get a Marine roster during those years around Ivan's birth. One thing we know is that he had intended to leave the military about ten years ago. So that narrows the scope of investigation quite a bit. But what I'm most concerned about is, what if he doesn't want to see the kid? I mean, do we explain to Ivan that he may be walking into a hornet's nest of some kind? I'm just not sure I can explain it to him."

"Maybe it isn't necessary to. We should find him first and ask him how he wants to handle it. I think we'll come to that decision in due time. Let's first see if he's alive, let's see if he's in the general vicinity, because we don't have the money to be traveling all over the United States to look for him, and let's see if he wants to talk to the boy. At the least, after they finish their investigation, he needs to be told about her death. I go either way about letting him know he's fathered a child. I sort of think it also needs to be up to Ivan for that."

"That's good advice."

Later on that evening, as Mia was cleaning up the kitchen and getting the kids put to bed, Fredo called Kyle and gave him the news about the Marine and Ivan's mother. He put the phone on speaker so Mia could listen in.

"That's a damn shame. Man, this kid has been living under a thunder cloud for a long time too. The last thing we want to do, of course, is get him in some kind of temporary place and then have him yanked out or come into some bureaucratic snafu somewhere where he's bounced around a bunch of times. This is a type of situation where he's too young to be making important decisions about his living situation. And the way our government works, it's not going to be good on him at all to sit around and wait. But I think the worst thing for me is the father. I think he's a jerk. And the kid deserves something better, doesn't he?"

"Amen to that, Kyle," said Mia to the phone receiver.

"You heard that, Kyle?"

"Loud and perfectly clear."

"He does deserve more. Much more," Fredo agreed.

Kyle reacted. "Now don't go taking that on yourself. The law is the law, and we are not going to interfere with how it's working. I think we need to stay out of it as much as possible but just be informed where the process is. At some point, you're going to meet somebody who's going to give you the keys to the kingdom, how all this happened, someone on the Mexico side who knew the family. That will be valuable information, so even if we can't have much of a say in where he's placed, we'll have one more piece of the puzzle to help future orphans. It's not a perfect world, but damn, his family back home may want him back or, at the minimum, will promise to stay in touch. I think that's going to be really important for Ivan."

"I couldn't agree with you more, Kyle."

"So any more information on Caesar or the boys at school?"

"No, I guess they've not had any more interaction, or the gang boys are not going to school. It's somewhere between that and nothing. Even Ricardo told Mia in confidence that he thought that perhaps the situation with Caesar was blown out of proportion like Ricardo suspected. But we have to stay vigilant."

"You know, Kyle," Mia inserted. "Sometimes when the kids don't tell you things, it isn't that nothing happened. They just won't tell you. So we could be reading it all wrong."

"I got you. I'm on the same wavelength. It's too bad there aren't some good guys who we could get to help you, but we're still looking for a good attorney who is familiar with criminal work. I don't think you have to worry about a custody battle—I think you have to worry about your own public safety."

Fredo agreed. "You haven't seen the pool yet, Kyle. You should see how the yard looks, the gardens, and the flowers. It's just absolutely beautiful. You know, Kyle, it was a stretch to try to get that pool in last year, but I'm so glad we did it. And Mia's taken to gardening just like her mother. She's very happy there. I would sure hate to leave that behind or have to leave the community for our safety. But you know, Kyle, I'd do it if we had to."

"I understand. And hey, Fredo, thanks for keeping me informed. I'm going to be all ears if I hear anything, if I get contacted by somebody from the State Department or Homeland Security or our special agent friend, I'll make sure they let you know too, and I'll keep you in the loop as much as I'm allowed. That said, we're going to have to go in for a debriefing tomorrow morning."

"Fuckin' frijoles! Why did they wait three days? I mean, there's been so much that's gone on already."

"I don't know. You know Homeland Security's pretty busy these days. So I'd give them a little bit of slack. And the Navy? Well, the Navy's busy all the time, too. That never changes. No picnic there. I think the debriefing is mostly for Homeland Security, and they're probably the ones that triggered it. So you be ready with your facts—think about them tonight, and if they call me in the morning and say we got to come in, then we got to come in."

"Okay, but I got an appointment with Ricardo's administrator at school tomorrow at noon. We're going to be careful but have to give her a heads-up so that if something happens on campus we have somebody who's watching for that."

"Good idea."

After the phone call with Kyle, Mia pushed Fredo into the living room while she finished the cleanup of the kitchen and put in another load of laundry.

"Never-ending story of my life: laundry!" she whispered to herself.

She joined him while he surfed the channels looking for something they liked. She knew that Fredo didn't want to think about his debriefing tomorrow. He needed a little distraction, first with the TV and then a nice hot, erotic shower before bed. Well, maybe some play in there someplace, too.

While he was flipping through channels, he saw a news flash from the southern border in Texas where a large caravan of women and children had drowned in the Rio Grande River, all of them undocumented, and as Fredo put his face up to the screen, he thought he recognized some of the clothing on what was a drone shot of a couple dozen people floating in the water. The announcer was letting the public know that some of these had been intentionally murdered, gunshots to the head, and that most of them had no papers, so there was no way to identify who they were or who they needed to inform.

Fredo looked at Mia. "I think that's the group we saw. I think that's Ivan's group."

"Seriously, Fredo?"

Fredo grabbed his cell phone and put it to his ear. "I'm going to call Kyle again."

"Wait until the morning. You'll see him. Enough already, Fredo," she answered.

But she was too late.

"Hey, Kyle, call me back, or turn on the news. There's a story about a migrant group that drowned in the Rio Grande in Texas at the Texas border. I think you should get a hold of that footage, because I think I recognize some of those people. Not their faces but some of the clothing. Like there was this lady with this bright yellow skirt and a black sarong over her shoulders. I think I saw that in the crowd they showed on the news. You don't have to call me back, but see if you can get hold of that footage, and maybe it'll help Gutierrez nail that Ochoa butcher. Just trying to help out. Let me know if you want me to do anything else."

Mia knew that Fredo was keyed up, ready for action. It just seemed like the hits kept on coming. First, it was Caesar getting out of prison, then it was the harassment of Ricardo, then it was meeting Ivan, and now this, the death of all these innocent people. It was too much to handle, and two of those very important events directly affected her family.

And then she remembered, they had an appointment at noon to talk to Ricardo's director in addition to that already full plate. How was she going to keep a lid on all of this? And what would Sister Mary Margaret think about all these issues they were embroiled in?

She was going to take a soak in the hot tub, maybe have a little glass of something, and get good and sleepy before she tried to go to bed. Otherwise, she would be up all night with worry.

And maybe Fredo could help with that, which brought a smile to her lips.

CHAPTER 11

FREDO WAS SURPRISED to see Special Agent Gutierrez at the debriefing the next morning.

"I understand you've been to the hospital a couple of times to visit our boy. Is he giving you good information?" Gutierrez asked.

Fredo noticed Kyle turning and heading in their direction. "There's a lot to this, and we found out that apparently his father lives in the United States. He was a Marine, maybe still is, but he was a Marine at the time he and Ivan's mother were together. Apparently, they were on their way to try to find him."

"Well, that's kind of a shock, isn't it? It makes it pretty easy then. That's where his final destination will be."

Fredo was afraid of that assessment, and he had a pang in his gut about that working out.

"Sir, if I can insert myself here," Kyle began. "Fredo and I have talked about this, and he's ready to put together an application to formally adopt Ivan."

"Whoa, whoa, whoa! Total cart before the horse here. You guys are jumping the gun. You can't poach this kid. He belongs to an American citizen."

Fredo was extremely troubled by Gutierrez's opinion. Before he could stop himself, he'd winced. He was glad Kyle spoke before he could open his mouth and say something inappropriate.

"Sir, if I could explain something to you. This little boy has been trafficked and damaged. He's lost his mother and his younger sister. However, he does have relatives back in Mexico, older siblings. And I'm not sure if his stepfather in Mexico is still alive. But one of the things we're concerned about is that perhaps he was convinced to travel with his mother and sister when he really didn't want to. Fredo and I came to the conclusion that it might be best if we check out the Marine father first, if we can find him, and then based on that, go forward with whatever we're allowed to do."

"Well, you can turn in an application for adoption. I can give you the form, but I think the likelihood it will be approved is quite small. We generally don't like to split up families. We all know he'll have a better life in the United States, but he won't be with anybody he knows. If he can be with his biological father, well, that's a little bit better than having him be a complete stranger here. But I don't see that it's anybody's place to seek his adoption. Can you explain your thinking about this?" He was looking directly at Fredo.

"I think what Kyle's trying to say is that maybe his father isn't going to want him. And before he gets shipped to some location where he doesn't know anyone, he and I or a couple of men who were there the day of his rescue could research, travel, and speak to the father first and then do what Ivan and the father would like. The father has rights, and Ivan has the right to not be bounced around the system. Gutierrez, you know that happens a lot. And I want your promise that you aren't going to hand him over to an NGO."

Gutierrez raised his eyebrows and then whistled. "Well, I'll say one thing for you guys, you do your research. But I can promise that deal. I don't think we have to involve the agencies. Most of them are Catholic charities. I don't think we have to put them in charge. And if you guys on your own time want to go find Mr. Lover Boy here, I'm okay with that. I really would like to see the kid get somewhere he wants to be. It wouldn't be the first time that a father disavowed having a child out of wedlock. So let's just do that then. But as far as promising you can be first in line for an adoption, Fredo, I'm afraid I can't do that. But you can go ahead and apply, and then you'll be at the head of the line if that should change."

Fredo was okay with that, and he told Gutierrez so.

The briefing was called to begin shortly, only eleven of the twelve SEALs who went to Mexico were available for this. Randy and his wife had booked a cruise several months ago, and there was no clause for a refund due to cancellation. Fredo had thought it was overkill to ask the entire platoon to show up, but he figured there might be something else going on, and he'd find out soon enough.

Kyle walked to the front of the room as team members took their places in the conference room. Fredo sat next to Cooper.

"How's it going there?" Cooper asked him.

Fredo leaned back and stared at the ceiling. "It's complicated, but the kid seems to be healing pretty quickly. They have to go in maybe twice and fix a couple of things, but he's really a trooper, and he heals remarkably fast."

"I heard about his father. Dumbass Marine, huh?"

"Well, a lot of our regular Navy guys are the same way, in all fairness," Fredo answered him.

"That's affirmative. A few Team Guys as well. But I hope it gets sorted. And I understand you're trying to effectuate an adoption if you're allowed?"

"Yep. Mia is behind it 100%."

"And what about your boys? How are they going to feel about this?"

"Well, we're not going to tell them until we know for sure we have the green light. That's always best with them."

"And Caesar, you run into him yet?"

"Not yet. I'm hoping that he's changed his mind or changed his ways. Honestly, Coop, we have so much on our plate. I'm glad he hasn't shown up yet. But we'll be ready if and when he does."

"How's Ricardo taking it?"

Fredo chuckled. "This is a direct quote, 'I don't want to meet that sperm donor. He didn't care anything about me, and instead of being a father, he decided to live a life of crime and go to prison for it.' And that's an exact quote from my son."

"Yep. You got your hands full, that's for sure. Well, you give my best to your lovely wife, and we'll see if we can arrange the kids to have a get together here. We're overdue, Fredo."

"I'm sure my boys are going to be happy to spend some time with Gillian. They're just barely beginning to wake up to the opposite sex. It's funny as hell, Coop. It really is. What an awkward time for a young man."

"You mean horndog."

They both laughed at Coop's comment.

"You were pretty funny, Fredo, when you went after Mia. I died laughing every day. What were you thinking? But nobody could talk you out of it, and look what happened. Now you've got three sons, and you're itching to make it a fourth. I'd say that is some serious dedication, Sport."

"And it has nothing to do with my sperm count, does it?"

"Thank God. Boy, I sure got tired of hearing about how yours had dented heads. You fuckin' moron, excuse me, mentally-challenged horndog. And I rest my case."

Kyle asked the room for quiet. "We're going to be calling you in one by one unless there's something specific they're going to need to talk to you about, and they will let you know in advance that the interview might go longer, but I've been told that these exit interviews are going to be a half an hour or less, which means you can break off early for the weekend. So that nobody gets their panties in a wad, we're going to go alphabetically, but we're going to go from Z to A this time. So sit back, you can calculate where you'll be in that pecking order, but don't leave the building, please. And, when your name is called, you're going to see these two gentlemen over here." He pointed to two regular Navy guys, both wearing headsets and wired. Both looked extremely young. The kind of guys many of the SEALs had a problem with—always messing with the rules and how it affected their careers. He hated the little infractions they occasionally had to endure on base.

"One additional item I'd like you to comment on, unless they ask you not to, how many of you saw the news broadcast last night about the migrants drowning in the Rio Grande?" Kyle had raised his arm above his head, looking for others. Only three of the eleven saw the news post, which included Fredo.

"So you might be shown a picture and asked if you recognize any of the clothing or the people in that picture. And I'm going to warn you, it's a little graphic. We're talking dead people here. People who have traveled over great distances and put their lives on the line, risked everything for a chance at freedom in the United States, if they're legit refugees. If they're lucky, they get to where they need to go, to a relative or an acquaintance who can sponsor them. But the vast majority of them get dropped off in a location, sent to a particular house to work off a debt that they didn't pay when they started their journey. And if they don't pay it, some of them don't make it, or their relatives back in Mexico or wherever they're from get visited and often hit up for more money or ghosted. So look hard at the photographs and see if you recognize anybody from the scene we witnessed live in Mexico three days ago."

They started calling names, and Cooper crossed his legs and his arms, leaning back into the metal chair, making it squeak. Fredo thought he looked extremely uncomfortable with his long gangly arms and legs, but he didn't want to criticize.

"Are you going to tell him you're interested in adopting the boy?"

"I'm not sure yet. I want to see what they're about first. That may be a detail that has escaped them. I am going to mention Caesar, though. It's not exactly germane to this particular operation we're being debriefed on, but all the same, it's something I feel I should disclose."

When Fredo's name was called, he discovered that the interviewers were not up to speed with what had happened during their mission. They were clearly way over their head as far as knowledge of tracking Mr. Ochoa. Fredo gave his account of what went down and his role in uploading the photographs and wishing they'd had a speech-modified long distance mic to pick up their communications.

"Duly noted, Special Operator Chavez."

They went back over the scene where Ivan's mother was killed and had him retell the incident several times.

"You're absolutely positive it was Ochoa who shot the mother and the little girl?"

"All the way down to his fuckin' green lizard boots. Unless the intel we were given was false or fake. He likes killing innocent people who become examples of the consequences of not following orders. Gentlemen, I don't have a dog in this fight, but it's dangerous for all of this to be going on at the border. It doesn't happen every day, but it's risky for all our own citizens there. Anything I can do to help protect the innocent, well, that's my mission too. And those poor guards down there trying to manage the border, you ought to be giving them all medals. With the international-sized flavor of the problem, I can't imagine it's something they signed up for in the first place. It's, in fact, probably something they don't want to have to do again. Kinda like hitting a ninety-mile-an-hour pitch with a teaspoon, if you get my drift."

He was shown a blowup of the drone picture he'd seen in the newscast. "You recognize this or any of these people?"

"Well, luckily, you can't see it here, but the newscaster said a few of these people had gunshot wounds to the head. That would be Mr. Ochoa's style, or guys he trained. Which makes me wonder if this wasn't supposed to be their intended outcome. Might allow the cartels to raise their prices to guarantee the next caravan. Get them to pay extra for their safety. But that's just how it comes at me, fellas."

"Anything else?"

"I'm trying not to look at it, if you don't mind, but I do recognize this woman here with the yellow skirt. I saw her alive before Ivan's mother was shot in the head."

"Ivan?"

"The little boy we rescued. You read my report, no doubt?"

"Yes, yes. Anyone else?"

"No, except that the ratio of women and children to preteen males is about the same as we saw down there. I could definitively say it's the same group. And that now means they'll be looking for us next time we go down there, unfortunately. And they'll be looking for drones."

"Oh, there will be drones, for sure," the investigator added. "They have them too. They are well-equipped, well-funded, not like our border operation who has to beg for everything."

That's a fact!

Fredo agreed with the gentleman completely. "My point exactly."

"Anything else?"

Fredo leaned back in his chair. "Are you researching the connection between these coyotes and the gang activity here in San Diego? Because there is one. I'm sure of it."

"Explain, please."

"It's like every gang member down here has creds with these bastards in Mexico. They go and come freely, bring in whatever they want. Except now they bring it in in huge shipments, use diversion so everyone's scrambling to keep up with the traffic in one area, leaving another fully exposed. We've seen this dozens of times. Why isn't more done to crack down on that connection between the locals and these cartels?"

"Many of the cartel members, the higher-ups, are legitimate businesses that are licensed to be involved. They overtake weak NGOs. There's plenty of money to go around, as we discussed before. The criminal doesn't have the worry about funding or the jurisdictional red tape between agencies like we have. You ever see the movie *Fitzcarraldo*?"

"Not sure."

"About a Peruvian billionaire who brought a steamer over the Andes one piece at a time. Nobody thought it could be done. Sometimes the way we do things here feels a lot like that feat of the impossible. In real life, they actually did it. Here? Well, let's say we're working on it."

"Got it. Let's hope their better angels start showing up. We need some help. Everyone down there needs help."

"Roger that, Special Operator Chavez."

The other interviewer asked another question about local gang activity which gave Fredo the room to mention Caesar.

"My wife was married to one of these guys, when

she was a rebellious teen and thought it was cool to hang with them. She had no idea what they were really into. This guy, who went up for it and has recently gotten a sweet deal to get out early, he's walking around here, free as a bird. His minions attend some of the same schools our kids go to. Now I'm the stepdad to a child whose biological asshole father wants to come 'back into his life.' What a family man, huh?"

The agents wrote down Fredo's details. "We'll bring this to the local director's attention, pass it along to the station chiefs. You may or may not hear from them, but thanks."

Then he produced a card, passing it along to Fredo across the desktop.

"Joel Bluestein," he read. "You live here?"

"Between here and LA."

"Okay, well, I'll let you know if I can use a hand-up. I'd like to find him in the middle of some dirty tricks and send him back to prison," Fredo said.

"Or the source," Bluestein added.

"Come again?"

"Don't you guys use that term? Sending them back to the source, back to the ground? Their holy place?"

"Oh, yes. I have my non-Middle East hat on. Now I understand what you're saying. Yup, that applies too."

Fredo was relieved that the debriefing was without an edge, making him feel like the criminal instead of the guy saving everybody.

He was told to prepare for another visit down there within a week. That didn't set well with him. He didn't see Coop or Kyle and decided not to discuss it with anyone else for now. Mia would be terrified he would be gone soon.

When he got home, he found Mia just stepping out of the shower, getting ready for their noon appointment at St. Cecilia's. It was a refreshing change, a holiday for his eyes and his heart.

"You could go that way. I think it would shock everybody in the office."

She came over to him, dropped her towel, and allowed all her pink parts do her magic to his very engorged pink parts. Fredo was urgent, but Mia stretched it out so long he didn't have time for a shower himself. He wished he'd never made the appointment. But even while dressing, he still had a boner after a fairly serious romp on the bed.

Which was exactly what he needed.

CHAPTER 12

MIA AND FREDO sat across the desk from Sister Mary Margaret, the director of St. Cecilia's School, where all three of their children attended.

"I'm glad the two of you came in together. We always try to encourage both parents to come, that way we don't have any miscommunications. In this day and age of social media, written instructions, bombardment of the news media, TV, cell phones, it's odd to me the older I get how much difficulty we have in communicating with each other. And I think there's just no substitution for 'together time.' I used to have a counselor I spoke to on a regular basis. She was a friend as her child was in our school as well, and she used to call it 'just bumping around time.' So thank you."

She gave a sweet smile and studied both of their faces one by one and then back to the other.

"Sister, we're grateful for your time. And we thought about this quite carefully before we decided to make the appointment."

Fredo turned and watched Mia's expression as he continued.

"We've had an unusual situation in the blending of our two families, and while the twins are mine biologically, Ricardo is in every way my son as well, except he was fathered by a rather difficult man. This gentleman had gone to prison and has been recently exonerated."

"I believe I was made aware of this," Sister Mary Margaret agreed. "But go ahead, explain what I can do for you two today. And for your family."

Mia felt it was perhaps her opportunity to step in and take over what Fredo had started. She wanted to start with some admissions—things she wanted to get off her chest.

"Sister, I did not always live my life as a Christian woman. In fact, I wasted a lot of my youth chasing exciting, shiny objects, which landed me in quite a bit of trouble. And I am regretful of those years."

Mary Margaret interrupted her. "He who is without sin? From the Bible? I think we all can say we have trespassed, and a trespass is a trespass. There's no such thing as a hierarchy of good and bad trespasses. But I understand what you're saying. You're saying that you have changed and you weren't proud of who you were, but now I assume you feel like you're on the correct path. Is that correct?"

Mia was relieved that the woman was so easy to speak with. She also gave herself a red flag, Fredo's admonition not to share too much. Before she continued, she looked at Fredo to make sure he was in agreement and saw his gentle nod.

"Well, I thank you for that, and I'm really relieved at your attitude. So as I was saying, I made some mistakes, and as you know, God sends children into the world, and they are not mistakes, even though unfortunately we sometimes talk about them in that fashion. Like something we have to get rid of. That's not me. So while the relationship with my former friend was in all ways a mistake, Ricardo, my baby, was not."

"I understand. Quite a mature attitude, my dear," Mary Margaret said.

Mia took a deep inhale and hoped she was using the right words, but she knew Fredo would stop her if that wasn't the case. "Ricardo's biological father went to prison for, among other things, abuse we suffered at his hands. I was pregnant with Ricardo when he was arrested. I had been beaten, tied up, kidnapped, the whole nine yards. He was reacting to the fact that I wanted a different life for me and my baby, and it wasn't something he could accept. So now he's out, and something we thought was going to be a thirty-year sentence? Turns out the courts have reversed their decision, and he's only going to have served nine of those thirty years. Which means, as a minor, he wants to be part of Ricardo's life again. Now we've heard this from boys here at the school who are friends of Ricardo's or maybe not friends but acquaintances. We've also heard it from certain officials at the prison where Caesar was incarcerated, and we've heard it through several other sources, both Fredo and I have. So this is fairly well documented as accurate."

"And has he contacted you?"

"Well, not directly himself, which is how he operates. He gets people to do things for him, so he can claim plausible deniability. It's like he doesn't care if anybody else gets caught, as long as they don't tell on him. And he has told some younger brothers, who are kind of circling around the gang hoping one day to be accepted. Tthey are thirteen, fourteen-year-old-boys, and three of them attend this school. He's delivered to them a message for our son, Ricardo, letting us know that he wants to be a part of his life. And they have been—I'm looking for the word—it's not ridiculed but it's interfering with Ricardo's presence here at the school, in that he can't get away from them. And they're bigger and stronger, and they have the backing of their gang, which we obviously don't have."

"But I understand you probably have most of the SEAL community behind you," Sister Mary Margaret inserted.

"Well, yes, that's true as far as resources, but I'm sure you're aware that they can't be called to action just because of how they're trained for things in the United States. At least they're not supposed to. And I don't want to get my husband in trouble for anything he isn't supposed to get involved with. Having said that, I know what kind of a man he is, and in this particular case, we can't take a proactive stance. We can watch, and we can be vigilant. But there's nothing else we can do. Unless you could help us out Sister."

Mia hoped that her subtle plea was picked up.

Sister Mary Margaret glanced over at Fredo. "I think I understand Mia very well. What mother wouldn't be concerned in this situation? I'd like to hear your take on it, please."

"I have been involved in this situation ever since the beginning. I have been in love with Mia since before she even knew I existed. I met her through her brother, Armando, who is also a member of SEAL Team 3."

Sister Mary Margaret leaned forward, put her elbows on the desk, and created a church steeple with her fingers. Her wizened and wise look showed Mia that she had a backbone of steel. She noted that the director could be a valuable ally or a formidable enemy.

"Oh my, so your family is populated with all sorts of heroes then. Good for you!"

"As Mia has said, there are limits to what we can do here and remain an active Navy SEAL. However, when it comes to the life, the health, and safety of my family, I will not hesitate to do what's necessary. I don't expect anyone else to protect my family any better than I could. There are good police and fire rescue, sheriff's offices, staffing. There are good people out there that try very hard, but they don't have the training I have, and they don't understand perhaps the mindset of the pure evil that is this gentleman. And I've seen it over and over again in our missions overseas. Bullies, people who take advantage of others, men and women who like to flaunt their power, belittle others, and I've seen whole villages in Africa want to rise up and murder some warlord or leader who has been so horrible, but they're afraid to. So they use fear as one of their swords."

"There are plenty of messages in the Bible about that very thing. Fear is a powerful weapon. The bigger and more complicated society gets, the easier it is for individuals like that to hide out and not pay the consequences. So I think what you're telling me is you want to make sure your family is protected but not at the expense of your career."

"Exactly! I am so glad you said that. I was hoping

that you would understand," said Fredo.

Mia could tell from just the timbre of his voice how grateful he was.

Sister Mary Margaret paused for a moment, reflecting on all her seventy or eighty years, and then said, "Well, my life is very simple compared to yours, although I do have roughly 2400 sets of parents I have to deal with, plus 60 teachers and teachers' aides, and I think, at exact count, we have 1,200 students. Some of them are remotely schooled, of course, but in the school, we have almost 1,000. It's a big school and very successful. But even that doesn't compare to the complications and the social forces you have to survive in, Mr. Chavez. And I thank you and respect you for that. I am not qualified to be able to strategize and create a plan that would be nothing more than just a guess. But I do promise you that I will watch. I will be careful how I discuss Ricardo with the other teachers, but I will suggest that extra care needs to be taken to watch him, as well as your twins, but I just don't feel comfortable orchestrating some kind of a plan beyond that. And I'm just trying to be completely honest with you, Mr. Chavez. This is way outside my wheel well."

"Sister, it's very brave of you and honest to admit that. I think there are a lot of people out there that just would like to have a couple private SEALs in their back pocket they could go send out and get even with all their enemies. I can see you're not one of those, and I'm grateful for that as well."

Sister Mary Margaret gracefully bowed her head and put her hands back in her lap.

"This is what I think would be ideal. Without making it obvious, I would like a journal kept of interactions between Ricardo and this group of boys or anybody else that happens to waltz on campus. There is to be no releasing Ricardo to his father under any circumstances, and I don't care what kind of paperwork is shown, he is not to go with anybody but Mia or myself."

"We'll put that in writing, too," added Mia.

"Understood, and I will make sure to alert the yard duty as well as the teachers. No problem with that."

"Frankly, we don't think it'll be very long before Caesar does something that could wind him back up in prison. It's difficult to just have to wait that out, and we certainly aren't going to poke the bear, but that may be what we have to do. He is very well-schooled in how to handle police, administrators, and the court system. Most of these guys who are leaders are very bright. They're just evil as well. I don't expect that he will do anything to harm Ricardo. You need to know that Ricardo, and you can verify this with him if you like, doesn't want to have anything to do with him. So if being at the school is a safe space for our boy, we want him to have that and always be under the attention of people that are looking out for his welfare, not policing him or spying on him, but genuinely concerned. I think that needs to be explained to him, so that when he sees people watching him, he knows. I don't think he will take it the wrong way, but we came here just wishing to open everybody's eyes and awareness to the fact that we could have a problem. And if we don't, hallelujah!"

Sister Mary Margaret smiled and clapped her hands, loving that comment. "Hallelujah! Amen to that."

Mia asked a question she'd been wondering. "Is this something, this conversation we're having, is this something that you are compelled to tell the police about?"

"Well, if it was threats of violence or, you know, a kidnapping situation, if that were something that had been threatened, then yes, we would be compelled. I would also call you and let you know. I cannot interfere with the police doing their duty, and their duty is to keep this school and every child, every teacher, every parent, every staff member safe. I'm not going to second guess them, and I'm not going to order them what to do. But this conversation we're having right now is not something they need to be privy to, unless we admit that we've discussed the possibility that

Caesar will try to contact his son outside your home and this would be the logical place."

"I'm satisfied." Fredo reached into his pocket and handed Sister Mary Margaret his card with his cell phone on it. "You call me anytime you see anything that doesn't look right. And let me write Mia's cell phone on the back of that card please."

She returned the card to him, and Fredo added Mia's cell.

"I'm going to be out of the country again for a few days, maybe a few weeks. I'm going to check in with you. I can also leave you a message and just let you know when I'm gone. As far as when I come back, I won't have that information, and if I did, I couldn't tell you. And I couldn't tell you exactly when we're leaving except that it will be very soon."

"I understand. Where are you going?"

"Ah! Forgot that one. You see, that's part of my agreement with my boss. We can't tell anybody where we're going or how long we'll be there. That's a violation of my oath. But we will do our best to inform you when I'm gone, so that you understand and you take appropriate actions. In that case, you definitely need to stay in close contact with Mia."

"Well, I've taken some good notes, and I will go over these with my teacher liaison and also Ricardo's homeroom teacher. I'm not sure I need to tell others about it except perhaps our yard duty person, who is actually a teacher waiting to be hired, so she sees all the kids on a regular basis and probably is going to be someone I will rely on quite a bit when I ask questions. I'm excited to say that I have the full faith and support of just about every teacher here, so you'll find I can assure you their complete cooperation."

"Well, Sister, this has been a pleasure." Fredo stood and extended his hand. Sister Mary Margaret shook it very firmly. Mia also gave her a handshake but didn't squeeze her fingers blue like Fredo did.

CHAPTER 13

I T WAS NEVER easy to leave the family on these fogless early mornings in San Diego, and it was often considered by Fredo and his teammates the most difficult part of the mission. Nobody wanted to be away from their families for an extended period of time in harm's way, least of all the wives. The men understood and took the challenge, because it was what they were hired to do. But seeing the toll that it took on the children and the wives was something difficult for most SEALs if they were human.

But in this case, Fredo was exceptionally worried, and although it never bothered him before, this time it did. There was no set end date to his mission, and all kinds of things were being thrown at them. It made it hard to strategize, get a grip, maintain control over their home environment and the outcome of a possible confrontation with Caesar.

He knew why that was the case, and it wasn't something that he disapproved of, because that's the way the job rolled, but he disliked how it affected Mia and the fact that she wasn't sure from one day to the next when he would be available to come to her aid. And she was dealing with a lot of things this time.

On a normal day, the boys were often rambunctious. She'd gotten proficient at managing them by herself, but Fredo knew this was draining. She never complained, she rarely made some comments, and especially now, she was trying to be very respectful of Fredo's feelings, a routine they followed before a dangerous deployment. These days, they all were dangerous. It was no ski trip to the Fjords of Norway or trekking across the red desert in Morocco.

They had woven together their highs and lows, their risks and rewards so many times as he'd been sent all over the world. While there wasn't anything such as routine with the Team, she was more used to it than she was in the beginning. And if complaints were going to be made, they had to be made after he was home, after the job had been done or not done, depending.

"I will try to call. You know the drill."

He hated to tell her that, but it was necessary.

"Yes, I do. Now once you step onto that plane and once you fly away from me, your job, Fredo, is to not worry about me and the kids. Your job is to get your butt home safe. I want you to think about that every moment that you're awake. And maybe in your dreams too."

He pulled her to him and hugged her, chuckling. "I can't wait. I'm already homesick for you." He pushed the hair out of her forehead and kissed her there, then on each cheek, and then hard on the lips. He tried never to think of it, but he knew he was joined by all the other SEALs who were saying goodbye to their wives and girlfriends or parents, that maybe this was the last kiss he'd ever have. Those had been things that happened in their community. God forbid it should happen to them.

"I love you, Fredo. Please, I'll be fine, pay attention to what you need to do and then get home safe. I mean that with my full heart. And I promise to let you know if something major occurs over here. But until you hear that, don't worry and don't wonder, okay?"

He smiled back at her, feeling all those warm, wonderful feelings he'd been having especially these last three or four days. She'd been unusually affectionate, cooking his favorite meals and doing all his favorite things in the bedroom. There were several times he was almost reduced to tears, he had been so moved by how caring and loving she was. She was nothing like the woman he met over ten years ago, a spitfire, smart and gorgeous, with a body that could stop a battleship, start a war even, unflappable, and yet inside still a little girl.

Now he was seeing the melding of that little girl and that saucy tart who would never give in to him and who honestly wanted him to just go away and told him so many times.

Now that melding had formed her into a warrior princess he had never imagined. She was fierce, loyal, and mean if she needed to be, but compassionate. And he could tell she loved being the woman she was, which meant she loved being his wife. And nothing in the world felt so good as having her to come home to.

"I am the luckiest man in the world, Mia. Who would've thought?"

She buried her head in his chest, and when he began to feel the tears stain his jacket and then his shirt underneath and then his undershirt, he knew she was just as moved as he was.

THEY ONLY SPENT an hour in the airport, because they were waiting for several Navy personnel, mostly ground support teams, who were bringing specialized equipment. There was a senator who was flying down there to discuss some situational things with their Spec Ops Lieutenant Commander who was stationed in Cabo San Lucas temporarily.

And there were also a couple of ladies who didn't identify themselves but appeared to be CIA or interpreters. They weren't State Department, because they would've shown their badges. So he guessed CIA. And he didn't know exactly what they were there for, but it was all part of the normal operation. This time they substituted the SEAL that couldn't go with another fellow on the team, Casey. He was a newbie, been in about six months, but was already skilled as a medic in training. Coop had been very impressed with him and had worked with him carefully.

Once they uploaded into the plane and took their seats, Fredo relaxed, closed his eyes, did some breathing exercises, and meditated, looking for that little spot at the very edge of the ocean, that place between the turquoise sky and the navy-blue sea. That line. That place of no man's land where sky and water blended, and it was so small the naked eye couldn't see it. As he focused on that seam line in the universe, he cleared his mind of everything and just saw the sea and the sky.

He was conscious of his heartbeat and his breathing. He still heard rumblings from the plane's engine and the rocketing that sometimes happened as they lifted through a heat spike, but more or less for the next twenty minutes, he was able to complete a thorough meditation, clearing his mind of everything except where he was and what he was there for.

They arrived in Cabo San Lucas roughly four hours later, offloaded into a couple of vans, which was their standard procedure, and headed down the narrow roadway, looking to traverse up the peninsula and then across to the border just south of the State of Texas. It was going to take them all day to get there, but they would get there by dusk.

The route had been circuitous, just in case someone had been informed of their arrival. They didn't want anyone in the know to be able to alert the bad guys. It certainly made the trip longer and more boring, but the strategy was that usually their teams were only tracked until they landed and deplaned. In this case, if the cartels were aware of their presence, they would not expect that they'd take the long track to the interior of Mexico.

A villa had been arranged for them, which didn't suck compared to the cactus and dusty hideout and night they had to spend overlooking the compound Ochoa had erected. They were about ten miles away, camouflaged in the little tourist village of artisans and specifically silver and inlay-work artists. As they wandered through the village at night, moving in groups of four or five so as not to alert the town that twelve Navy SEALs had arrived, store after store, most of them closed, showed beautiful intricate artwork and craftsmanship. Money had been tight for Fredo and Mia after the decision to put the pool in, but Fredo wanted to buy her something and found a pair of silver hoop earrings with a tiny etching looking like a flower vine all around the rim. He thought that looked like her. He made a note to come back and get it for her if it was reasonable.

He texted Mia to let her know he'd arrived safe and would be off the waves for a bit and to wait for his call to her.

They settled down for the night, but before they fell asleep, Kyle laid out what their plan was for the next day. He rolled out one of his famous maps, marked up and wrinkled. It was like the bible of what they'd been doing down there the past three or four years. Almost like a journal, except it was a map. It helped their orientation, especially with the new tadpoles.

"So we're here, and Ochoa's compound is right here, if you recall. We are going to just take it light the first day. We're not going to do any stealth night stuff for maybe a couple of days, and that's because we might find something we need to further inspect. So we're going to be casually watching this compound as we drive past it to another village, and we're going to be posing as business people, scouting for a remote location to perhaps build a factory. That's the story. Now don't get too detailed if you talk to the locals, because someone will blow it and say something that the rest of you aren't going to know, and then we're going to get discovered. They're watching for that."

To a man, everyone nodded understanding.

"But they aren't going to suspect you too much if you're looking to start a business in Mexico. They want the work, they want to be your conduit, and it's not politics for them; it's money. So we are not a threat to the common people, only to the gangsters and criminal elements. But mind you, every single person you're going to meet has a connection to a cartel member. It's just impossible to get away from them. You don't want to talk too much about this fictitious business. You want to make it sound like just formulating ideas and looking at different communities, and you can ask questions about the community and then focus on what you really want to know. That would be reasonable. But if you, of course, walk up to somebody and say, 'Hey, have you seen this bad guy Ochoa,' because everybody knows him, you'll immediately be reported. They'll be rewarded. More than likely, you'll be dead. Please remember that, and please keep your wits about you twenty-four seven."

There were a few questions, mostly from the newer guys, since the older ones knew that food would be brought in, as would happen if they really were businessmen scouting for a location. They would always keep their guns not visible in the house, and they would use their props that they were asked to bring. A few people brought fishing poles, others brought camera equipment, portable game machines, cards, and journals. They weren't going to look like the militia had just come to town. They were going to look like regular, straight businessmen looking for a partner in Mexico to do something that will help both sides.

"All right, let's get some sleep."

Fredo raised his hand. "Kyle, are we allowed to text home anytime? Or are we on emergency only mode?" He wasn't going to reveal he'd already done so.

"No, you can text. Keep it very short. Remember you're a player, so you aren't going to be tied to your wife's apron strings, right? So keep that in mind in case somebody's looking over your shoulder."

"Anybody else?"

"Are we going to be traveling with interpreters?" Riley asked.

"We elected not to this time. That usually requires a local person to be used, and this area isn't quite the population numbers so that we could do that safely and not have it get back to the cartels. But that doesn't mean you can't ask shopkeepers and people you meet down in the town square about places to go to eat or drink or buy gifts, that sort of thing. A business-class tourist would do that. And that was a good question, by the way. I was waiting for that, and then I forgot to mention it."

Fredo took a shower and righted himself for bed. He even shaved. When he came back into the room,

Cooper, who was one of the two guys he was sharing the room with, looked up from his book.

"Everybody good at home?"

"She hasn't responded yet. But I'm sure she has it all under control. Are you worried at all about this guy? I mean, he's got to have a sixth sense, being a former cop. I just hope we get some good credible intel from that drone right away, get in and get out. What say you?"

"Yeah, same here. It would be okay by me if we got to come home in a week or less."

"What are you reading?" he asked Coop.

"How to make a pistol out of Legos in a hurry. It's kind of cool."

"My favorite was the artificial mechanized arm we used in the Middle East. Remember that thing? You'd hold your arm out there, and all we'd see were asses and elbows."

"Yeah, and you, asshole, had a hard time keeping a straight face. Trying to get me killed?"

"Nah. A pistol would be easier. Night, Bro." Fredo turned his phone off, which still left a small alarm buzz in case of an emergency, laid back on the bed, and pictured that ocean and that sky scene one more time.

Until Coop ruined it by calling out in falsetto, "'Nighty-night, Princess."

"Fuck you," Fredo whispered as he rolled over.

"Not. My. Type."

CHAPTER 14

MIA'S PHONE RANG, and she was surprised to find Special Agent Gutierrez on the other end of the line.

"Is this Mia Chavez?"

"Hi, Agent Gutierrez. Fredo isn't here. He's on deployment. But can I help you?"

"Well, we processed your husband's application. It's in both of your names, for the adoption. At least we've put it on file, and the boy has, for now, finished the surgeries that are required. Tomorrow, they're going to release him from the hospital. I'm supposed to find a place to take him, and I remembered our conversation. Do you want to take him for a spell?"

"For a spell. What does that mean?"

"On a temporary basis. It could become more permanent. You'd get the first crack at him."

Mia was quickly not liking Agent Gutierrez' tone. But this was good news. She told herself to smile.

"Well, sure. Now is this a sure thing or is it maybe going to happen, because I'm going to have to talk to my kids."

"Well, I thought you guys had already decided that you wanted to do it. Now if something's changed—"

"No, sir, this is still the same. It's just that I didn't want to put the kids through too many changes, so we decided not to tell them until it was a sure thing. But there's no problem. I'll tell them today as long as you're sure that this is going to happen."

"Well, in our line of business, we never can be sure of anything. I'm sure Fredo can relate to that."

Mia felt slightly insulted at his attitude.

"Have you ever tried to raise three boys on your own? I do it all the time, and the six or so times a year when Fredo's gone, he's not available to tell me how to work the washing machine or get the internet working, or who I should take the TV to or what happens if the car is sending colorful lights in my face."

"Okay."

Now Mia felt he was annoyed with her.

"Look, I will be happy to take Ivan, and I think what I'll do is take all the kids over to the hospital. Can we do it that way? They won't be in school tomorrow."

"I'll arrange it. You know the room he's in, right?"

"Of course."

"And you'll inform your husband?"

"Oh, heck, no can do. I was going to make it a surprise."

"Well—."

"It was a joke, Agent Gutierrez. I'll do it right now. I may only be able to leave a message. But he usually calls every day if he can, and if he can't, I usually shouldn't be calling him. But no worries. We'll handle it. What time should I be there tomorrow?"

"Well, they say they release at 10:00, but I am going to say why don't you pick him up right after lunch? Then he can get a good meal, and between 12:00 and 1:00, if you come at that time, he should be ready to go. He's going to move a little slow, because he's got a cast and a sling, and you know, he has to have help showering and all of that."

"Okay, so do I need to get anything to cover his shoulder or make sure it doesn't get wet?"

"I'd check with the nurses tomorrow."

"Thank you, and is there a checkout process or something I have to sign?"

"It'll all be there for you tomorrow. If I can, I'll come over. I may not be in town that day, though. But you have my cell. This is my direct line to my cell, and call me if there's any kind of a problem. And I want to thank you. I was going to have to spend four or five hours finding a home for him, since I promised both you guys he wasn't going to be taken to Catholic

Charities. They are pretty good, you know, not all of them are bad, but boy, we have some bad agencies out there popping up all over the place."

"Well, that's because they smell the money."

Mia continued to be irritated at the special agent's sloppiness as far as handling details. It was quite obvious to her that he would never be the right kind of a parent to stay home with the kids, especially three boys who liked sports and wanted to do all sorts of extracurricular activities. Mia knew that many SEAL marriages were destroyed by the fact that there was this hierarchy, everybody was looking up to and admiring the SEAL members themselves. Meanwhile, the wife was at home running the show most of the time, except for when he got home and was Mr. Big Cheese again. She'd never had that problem with Fredo, but she'd heard others complain, and she agreed with it pretty much. This guy, Mia knew that he would not be a very compassionate partner. Maybe that's why he was still single.

Mia called Fredo's number and got the standard voicemail stiff arm. She left a message, even though there was a fifty percent chance that it wouldn't take. Then she called Christy Lansdowne.

"Oh my god, that's great news, Mia. Does Fredo know?"

"Well, I can't get a hold of him, I assume he's in

place and can't answer, but if he listens to his messages or if you talk to Kyle, tell him to let Fredo know he's got a message, okay?"

"You bet. So you pick him up tomorrow at the hospital, is that what it is?"

"Yes. We're going to get there around noon. I'm taking all the kids."

"Well, if you need to drop them off here, if that's something you want to do on your own, you and Ivan face-to-face, then you could take him home and show him the house. If that's what you want to do, I'm available tomorrow. I'm not working."

"Well, I suspect you've got a house full of kids then."

"Yeah, we do. And I've got a couple I'm waiting to hear from, supposed to be a play date trade off, but you know how that goes. People get busy. It might just be my three. So drop them by if you need to."

"Thanks, Christy. I think I'm going to stick with my plan. My goal was to try to bring him into the family and let everybody be involved in that process, and the kids are pretty good about their behavior, especially in a hospital where things have to be quiet. I don't even know if they'll let them in the room. Sometimes they don't."

"Yeah, you're right about that. Some floors have strict rules about it."

"But we'll sort it out. I mainly just wanted you to know so that Kyle did, because if Fredo was here, Kyle would be the first person he'd call."

"I got that, thanks."

Mia had some of her mother's fresh tamales frozen in the garage, so she took them out, covered them, and left them in her refrigerator to thaw. She thought Ivan would enjoy those, but she didn't know what kind of food he liked. She made a list of a few things her kids liked and made some guesses on Ivan's behalf. She headed out to pick up things at the store nearby.

Then she remembered the twins had soccer tomorrow morning. It was a highly anticipated game, and they wouldn't want to miss it.

She telephoned the coach and asked if the game was still on and if the boys could miss it. She got an earful about the commitment his players' parents had to make to either play or go home.

"I've got an issue with transportation. I have some place I must be between twelve and one. Could you perhaps pick up the boys on your way to the field?"

"I'll have Mrs. Spencer do it. She's the Team Mom. I'll have her call you. This number?"

"Yes, please."

"Okay, calling her next. You let me know if it isn't arranged, and we'll figure something else out."

"Thank you, Coach Smith. I really appreciate this."

Julie Spencer called and agreed to pick up the boys at eleven in the morning. "It's a shame you are going to miss the game."

"Maybe I can drop by and see the end of it. But, if I don't make it, could you either take the boys to your house for a few minutes before I get there or drop them off at my house? I can try to get a sitter."

"Oh, nonsense. I'll bring them home if we don't see you. But this is such an important game!"

"I know. But I have to do an extremely large favor for someone. It came up last minute, and I'm so sorry."

"My, you certainly have a busy life, Mia."

"Fredo's on deployment. He's just left. I'm all alone."

"I understand. I'm happy to help out. Hope we see you tomorrow."

So that had changed the trajectory for tomorrow. Mia decided she'd pick up Ivan after she saw the boys off safely. Ricardo would want to stay with them and watch. But she'd let him choose. Perhaps he'd want to meet Ivan first. Either way, it was all set.

Everything had happened so fast. She hoped she didn't leave something out. She recounted each step of her plan and couldn't find any holes.

With the possibility another child would be coming to live with them, she was going to have to establish a routine, stick to it, and get the rest of the family to help her out. And maybe she'd need some special help from her mother and Gus.

Her phone rang, and once again, it was Gutierrez.

"Something's changed?" she asked. "Or am I suddenly your most favorite person?"

"I'm sorry. I've just been informed the application was denied."

"Wait a minute, you told me it never really was posted, just filed."

"Apparently, I was wrong. Now, I have a way you can still take Ivan, since all my initial instructions were to have CPS come get him tomorrow afternoon at Scripps. I've just talked to his doctor, and if you can get there this afternoon, say close to noon, would you be able to take him home today?"

Mia thought it was odd all of this had been so disorganized and poorly planned. And she was doing all the adjusting.

"H-how come, if our application was denied, I am given permission to take him home today? Why is one day make that kind of a difference?"

"Bureaucracy. That's all I can say. I'm really sorry. The excuse that the paperwork just crossed paths, adjusting the timing, is always a good one."

"Who is making these decisions?"

"It's DHS. And you are quite correct, it's all messed up, very fluid, and changes all the time. We're in full panic mode here, and it's getting worse. I only wish there were more wonderful people like yourselves to help. We are starved for those resources."

"Well, I have to pick my kids up at school at two. There better not be a delay when I get there, or you will have to find someone else."

"I promise. If I have to go over there myself and make it happen, you'll be able to pick him up at noon. Where are you now?"

"Why?"

"Just didn't want you to get there before I get the signoff delivered to the floor."

"I'm on my way to the store to pick up some things. Then I'll head over. I'm not far."

"As long as it's not before twelve. You might see me there begging the head nurse. It won't be pretty."

"Agent Gutierrez, I'm not doing anything illegal, am I?"

"No. Why would you say that?"

"Well, everything about this plan seems like a leaky boat. Now you might have to beg to have Ivan discharged today? I didn't think hospitals operated this way? I don't want to get caught up in some issue and have CPS after me or—"

"Mia, you have a very active imagination. Stop making yourself crazy."

Now she really didn't like his condescending tone.

"Maybe you should let Ivan go into the system like all the other kids."

She couldn't believe that she'd just said that, but she had a knot in her stomach that was growing. All she saw were problems ahead, and no one to help her solve them.

And then she remembered the face on that little boy, the one who had seen his mother and sister murdered. Maybe she was being overly critical. Maybe this sort of thing happens this way, and perhaps that's the reason everything isn't working right now. Her guilty conscience was kicking her in the shins.

And then Gutierrez delivered the final blow.

"All he has is you, you and Fredo. You two have the biggest hearts of anyone I've seen. But I understand. You have limits. You're not used to this. So let's just forget it—"

"No. I'll pick him up. But you better have him ready. I've just rearranged my whole day tomorrow, I've asked for special favors to pull this off, and now I have to redo everything. But you're right, what Ivan is going through is far worse. But please have him ready. No problems."

"Fine. We'll be ready for you, then. Don't rush. You want to be safe. And thank you for your kindness."

Mia was liking agent Gutierrez less and less the more she talked to him. She wouldn't have anything to do with him if it weren't for Ivan. She decided to overrule her gut and go with the plan. She glanced at the clock and saw she had plenty of time, if she didn't dally. Luckily, there wasn't traffic yet for a Friday. She hoped Fredo would be pleased with her decision and that he was safe, wherever he was. She started to rehearse what she was going to tell the boys.

Just before she came upon the entrance to parking, she checked her rearview mirror. She noticed the same black car had followed her from the corner of her street all the way to the parking lot of the grocery. He must have realized he'd been spotted, because he parked several rows away from her and didn't exit the car. She thought he looked like an undercover policeman, maybe somebody from immigration, DHS, she didn't know. But whoever that person was, they were in some kind of official capacity. No uniform, no specialized plates, just a feeling she had.

She made a ruse of having to get one of the long carts which was stuck in a row of baskets near his car. As she headed over to the cart station, she kept her phone in the palm of her hand as if she was trying to hold it while she was steering the cart. She tried to take several pictures and then switched it to video to take sweeping videos as well. When she got home, she would research the license plate and phone it in to Gutierrez. Maybe she should call her stepdad Gus

Mayfield too. Anyway, she had to get a good description of the car, the license plate, and the guy in it.

Taking the cart and making a big U-turn, heading for the front door of the market, she was surprised to hear the car door open and a man's voice call out to her.

"Ma'am? Can I bother you for a second?"

She whipped around and looked at him. He was dressed casual but nice. It still didn't give her a warm fuzzy feeling to get very close to him. She stood behind the cart so that there was eight to ten feet between them. Her hand still operated the video feature on the cell phone, and she pretended like she didn't know it was on and looked for a place to store the phone but didn't have pockets. She didn't want to alert him that she suspected something.

"What do you need? Stay right there, please."

"Are you Mia Guzman?"

She froze in place, then whipped around, ditching the cart and sending it back toward the stranger, and ran to the front of the store. She could tell he was coming after her, the sounds of his shoes scraping across the paved parking lot was unmistakable.

She got to the doors before he did, but they did not close as fast as she'd hoped, and he was able to run through at the same pass she did. She ran to the first teller she could find. The lady always wore too much makeup and had bright red hair and painted-on eyebrows and lips that pursed in a perfect heart shape, looking like some kind of a morph between Cruella de Vil and the Wicked Witch of the West. She was already made up for Halloween; every day she looked like that.

The clerk's eyes grew large as she saw Mia in pursuit by this rather beefy guy running full tilt toward her.

The assistant manager thought he was taking good care of his other customers in the store and came over nicely to get Mia to slow down. He got between Mia and the guy in the parking lot, and they both tumbled to the ground.

The teller whispered to Mia. "Go to the office. The manager's there, and they'll call security."

"Thanks."

She knew where the office was, right next to the women's bathroom, and she'd been in there quite a few times with all three boys. She barely got through the door when the gentleman from the parking lot showed up, right behind her. And then the assistant manager behind him, holding his nose, bleeding down the front of his shirt.

"Call the police." Mia said.

The office assistant took too long to figure it out, and by the time she had picked up the phone, the parking lot dude had ripped it out of her hands and thrown it against the wall. In a big beefy voice, he yelled at all of them, "Somebody close that fucking door. You!"

He pointed to the bloody assistant manager.

"Nobody else move, and I want to see everybody's hands on their laps or on a desk somewhere."

Then the worst of the worst happened, he pulled out a pistol. It looked like Fredo's SIG Sauer.

"The first person to disobey me is going to get shot. You don't want to be that person."

The other two office helpers as well as the general manager himself walked in through an anteroom office in the back, completely uninformed as to what was going on. They quickly complied. When the general manager didn't know what to do with his hands, the fellow from the parking lot told him to face the wall and place his hands on either side of his ears.

Mia just stood there. And looking down at her palm, she saw that the camera was still rolling.

"Thank God," she whispered to herself. Unlike her pretense, she did have a pocket in her jeans, and quickly stowed the phone in front, hoping the man would not find it if she was alone with him. She needed that evidence, and she was going to do everything she could to protect it. It had his description, the license plate number, the make and model of the vehicle, and now all these threats. Everything they needed to find and detain him.

"This little lady and I are going to take a ride. And I'm going to count to fifty, because I think she looks pretty fast, so if we run, I think we'll make it in time. I don't want anybody here calling cops or security."

Right on cue, they heard banging on the door that the assistant manager had closed and locked. The two managers looked between themselves and somehow the message was relayed that the assistant manager should just unlock the door quickly and then duck. Because that's exactly what he did in the next movement.

The fellow from the parking lot raced to the other side of Mia. He shot the assistant manager in the chest twice and then grabbed Mia's arm before the security guard and several other tellers behind him could even enter the doorway. By waving his gun and grabbing Mia around the shoulders and neck with his other arm, he was a formidable character, and no one anyone would want to tackle. Mia heard screaming echoing off the walls of the store as people panicked.

They made it to his car. He opened the passenger door and threw her inside. She locked the windows and doors and tried to honk the horn, but without the ignition on, the horn was ineffective. She looked for something to break the windows and found another revolver in the glove box. She checked it, and it was loaded. She released the safety, and when the gentleman came to the driver's side, he got blasted in the chest through his driver's window and fell backwards into the carts.

Mia scrambled out of the vehicle. A group of bystanders encircled her and the man who was shot. She raised her arms and placed the gun on the hood of the car.

"He tried to kidnap me. This is his gun. Somebody, please call the cops. Please."

She felt lightheaded and woozy and wasn't quite sure where she was for a second. Disoriented, the parking lot started to rise up in the middle and presented an angled look. Everything was out of focus, sharp angles everywhere, people's faces were blurry, and she felt sick to her stomach. But the last thing she remembered before she blacked out was seeing the guy struggling in the carts, flailing, his arms and legs working, but with a huge wound in his abdomen, he wasn't going to be running anywhere.

"Asshole," she thought to herself before she passed out.

CHAPTER 15

ONE OF THE things Fredo learned early on in his naval career was that what was constant was inconsistency. Things could change in a moment, minute, an hour, or a day. They would go through a long dry spell with nothing to do basically, and then all of a sudden, it's like everybody woke up and took a dose of adrenaline, and the world started exploding again. That's when they were needed the most.

So when they saw the orders come through early in the morning, Kyle got them up at four and went over what task they'd been given. They had drone footage of several large vehicles, including one semi with a huge trailer, heading toward the compound where Ochoa was. It was believed, based on the intel they had sent back last time they were here, that they were transporting several hundred human prisoners to some kind of a crossing, and that crossing could have been anywhere along the Texas to California border. They could use drones, but there might be the opportunity to nab Ochoa, and that was what the SEALs were there for.

Fredo wasn't too worried about the mission, since they were obviously more trained than anything he'd seen so far of Ochoa's militia. But anything could happen, and with a trailer full of human cargo, it made rescue a little more difficult but not impossible.

Kyle had put a strict lockdown on all their cell phone use, which annoyed Fredo, since he was dying to check in with Mia. He also knew that if there was something critically important at home, somehow they would get him the message.

Everyone geared up, got their night vision equipment ready, and then also got their day packs stored in separate duffel bags. The two vans they had, both of them with the logo of a pleasure vacation outfit that was a legitimate tourist representative near Mexico City, was their cover. They did not use any local drivers, but Armando and Fredo, since they were native speakers, would be driving and act as tour guides if they were pulled over.

So before sunrise, they got in place near where they had spent the night before and watched carefully as the large semi pulled in through the massive gates of the compound. Behind the semi were three all black Suburbans.

With his night vision lens, Fredo was able to take

fairly closeup pictures. However, the black tinting on the windows made it impossible to identify who was inside there. He took pictures of all of the guard stations on the outside of the compound, the turrets that were guarded inside, the guards crossing back and forth across the courtyard, which served also as an equipment staging grounds and turnaround, and the guards maintaining order in the cages that were open to the elements, tarps thrown over them in the hot part of the day. It was squalid conditions, humans being kept like zoo animals. Add to the fact that several of them were young children, it sickened Fredo's stomach.

Barely an hour transpired before one of the black limos took off from the gate, and after checking with the powers in San Diego, it was determined that the SEALs should stay in place and not go after what could be a decoy. They would find out soon enough if Ochoa had made his escape with the first Suburban, and if that were the case, well, there still was the issue of where they were taking the semi and how they could interdict and stop them, so that any hostages inside could be freed.

Fredo knew Kyle was calculating every scenario, even the almost impossible scenario that all this was a decoy or diversion and what was really going on was some main operation elsewhere.

As the light of day descended upon the compound, what became evident was that the semi-truck was not bringing human cargo, but bushels and bushels of drugs. White plastic bags were loaded into the back, floor to ceiling. Fredo couldn't tell if it was farm supplies, flour, or sugar. So possibly, Ochoa had negotiated a deal to expand his operation to include drug trafficking in addition to human trafficking. It was unlike him, and with the way he reacted to drugs being given to him as payment for passage, it sort of surprised Fredo. But he let it be.

Instructions were given to follow the large truck, even if it meant not following Ochoa. It was thought that this was an even greater prize, and since it had entered and exited the Ochoa compound, it could contain proof enough that he had expanded his operation and might be enough to get the Mexican government to capture him and turn him over.

That was the theory. Now came the execution.

As the semi pulled out of the gate, the team noticed that the two blacked-out Suburbans remained behind.

"Boy, that's odd. It's just not like what I expected at all," said Kyle.

"You think it's a trap?" Cooper asked.

"I don't know. I just never know with these guys. You know that the average lifespan of a cartel head is less than five years after they join?"

"You're kidding," said Fredo.

"Nope. They get involved, and they get used up. It's like fish eating the fish eating the fish, and finally, the whale gets them all, right? You've seen that cartoon."

"Oh, yeah. So what are we doing? Which fish are we?" Fredo asked.

Kyle looked through his binoculars again. "They're still in the cages. They don't look like they're getting ready to be transported, and with all those bags, it's almost like this is a warehouse. A truck's here to pick up goods and then deliver it to wherever. My hunch and my guess is perhaps somebody paid Ochoa to be giving them safe passage across the border, using one of his routes and all of his guys. And they told us to expect to find his guys on both sides of the border."

"Yeah, saw a program once they've infiltrated the police in LA and San Diego. Can you believe it? Gang members and cartel bosses as cops?" Coop said.

"If I can get closer, I could probably get license plates, maybe make out some faces. What do you think?" Fredo asked.

Kyle shook his head. "Nah, it's not that important. I think we just go when they say to go."

Kyle spoke into his INVISIO and gave the team orders to prepare themselves to leave on a moment's notice. The day camp was pulled down, all the supplies stored back in the vans. All evidence that they had ever stayed there was removed, even to the point of someone doing one last sweep with large branches tied to his feet, swishing over the rocks and sand and small cactus brush, even removing tiny pieces of paper with tweezers, paper that the SEALs probably never left. But except for the tire tracks, which they could do nothing about, everything was put back into its original position.

Finally, they got the orders to track the truck. A whole fifteen minutes had gone by, and no further action was seen from the compound. Coop had launched his drone carefully and notified Kyle that the truck was headed straight for the highway west and did not meet up with any other vehicles. But it was coming to a major village.

"Before we take off, can you run it by the compound, the prisoner area there?" asked Kyle. "I want to get some pictures, and they probably won't be good enough for facial recognition, but they might be able to digitally recognize people that have been reported missing or we know have been kidnapped. I'd like to be able to send that off before we leave."

Coop responded, "Will do. I'm on it right now."

Coop always scrunched up his mouth while he manipulated the bird, like how somebody would stand and move and make noises while they were using a pinball machine. If you jerked the machine around too much, of course, it would tilt, but people tried to do it anyway and never affected the outcome of the game. Coop was using his extra-long neck, his six-foot-four-inch frame and long fingers to arch himself, push forward and back and bite his lower lip when he placed the drone close to the perimeter of the compound, hovering just far enough out of eyesight. He even let it hover behind a tall pine tree that had been partially denuded, getting shots of the compound from two angles that they couldn't see from their lookout. All the footage, and there was quite a bit of it, was uploaded. Kyle was on the phone while he looked at Cooper's monitor, discussing what they found with one of the officers back in San Diego.

"Yes, sir, we're ready to go whenever you let us know. The truck's got about a twenty-minute advance on us, but Coop's drone has determined that they haven't hooked up with anybody else, and they are on their way to the highway. My guess is they're going to enter Texas or someplace remote."

He listened while he was given instructions. Nodding his head, Kyle signed off.

"So we're to follow. How much life do you have left in that bird, Coop?"

"Oh, I got about six hours maybe. I've got the rapid recharge, though. All I need is about thirty minutes of downtime and she's good to go again. What's the question for?"

"They want us to just follow but not be detected. We have to follow enough behind them so they don't see us. And we're to look for drones when we get to the Managua Flats village. That's when we need to close the gap and pay close attention to where the truck goes. It's possible it'll be offloaded to another vehicle. I really don't know. But we're to watch and report."

"Okay, got that."

Kyle again turned on his comms, notified San Diego they were leaving, and then gave instructions to his men to load up in the vans in the same order they came in and get ready for a several-hour drive.

About an hour later, the truck started to speed up, and if they hadn't had the drone, they would've missed the fact that the truck turned off just before the village. It rounded a small mountain that looked more like an extinct volcano crater. In the next few minutes, all they could do was follow the curve of the road around the mountain, heading the opposite direction of the village. The roadway then traveled straight north, toward one of the border crossings.

"Son of a bitch!" Fredo said. "Where the hell is he?"

Several of the other team members in Kyle and Fredo's van swore openly. Everyone was searching the horizon everywhere, and there was no trace of the vehicle.

"It just disappeared into thin air?" Kyle said. "Did you get drone footage, Coop?"

"I got nothing, Kyle. She went for the village. I'm calling her back." Then he had an idea. "Why don't you head back the way we came, and I want to take a look at the side of the hill. We might have missed something."

There being no other vehicles on the three paths they could take, for as far as their eyes could see, they agreed and turned around and headed back in the direction of their villa. As they rounded the curve, which is where they lost the truck, everybody looked out the left side of the van. What was almost perfectly camouflaged was a large seam in the mountain, an actual door made of stone, even planted with trees, and apparently they had some kind of mechanism to open that door and store the truck inside. The fact that they had followed, lost the truck, and then come back and found the entrance probably meant that the team had been discovered as well.

Kyle notified San Diego about what had occurred and asked about their surveillance. He was told they had missed the pass of a satellite overhead, so had no record of the vehicle turning off anywhere. Kyle was given orders to return to the villa.

Fredo wondered why they would go back to that villa, especially if they were suspecting that they'd been discovered. Perhaps they were going to be readying for a firefight as maybe the militia from the compound mobilized and were going to greet them when they tried to arrive. Or they could get there and find everyone gone, including the prisoners that they all had seen.

There were so many things that could have happened, and he wondered also why all of a sudden the operation had changed from something that had been done day in and day out, practically like clockwork, into a rather unusual operation involving a semi that drove into a mountain for camouflage. And if they were going to be selling the material in the back of the trailer, why would they hide out in a mountain?

Coop let the drone fall back so they'd be notified if some convoy came from the direction of the semi to overtake them. It was dead as dead could be. In fact, there weren't even any animals out prowling around, dead ones either on the roadway. That was very unusual.

They made it all the way to their compound, but before traveling up the private drive, Kyle directed Fredo to turn off and take a back road where a small hill would give them a good view of their compound and Ochoa's in the distance.

"You're thinking we just need to wait a bit and see what turns up? Are we playing like bait now?" Fredo inquired.

"I don't know what's going on, but I certainly don't want to put you guys down in the middle of it there. I mean, there's no cover. They could bring in jets for all I know. It could be rigged to blow up. I just think we better stay here where we know Ochoa comes back to very frequently and watch what he's doing and not go chasing off after black Suburbans and large semis. And now I'm wondering what's in those bags?"

Danny piped up and added his two cents. "You know, they could have been bags of fertilizer, Ammonium Nitrate, like the stuff they make bombs out of? My uncle back in Arizona puts bags of that stuff on his farm, trying to get his fallow field to grow, but it has to be applied constantly every year, and they go through a ton of it. Maybe that's what it is. Maybe it's just for farming or maybe it is for bomb-making."

"Interesting," Kyle said.

"You know, Kyle, if they were making bombs, that would be the perfect place for them to do it. I don't think there's anything that could penetrate that mountain, as far as radar, and except for the few times when the truck's going in or out, it just looks like a normal hill, very expensively put together," noted Coop.

"So we're thinking maybe it's a bomb factory, not a delivery to the US?" asked Fredo.

Several of the guys agreed with this assessment.

"I'm going to run that up the ladder and see what they say," said Kyle.

Fredo pulled up into a small thicket of trees barely taller than the van and a large flat area next to it, covered with tire tracks, where he could park and they could surveil their own digs. Kyle motioned for him to stop while he talked to his LT back in San Diego.

"Sir, we've kind of looked at how all this feels to us, and I'm just going to float a suggestion or a what-if in front of you. You tell me what you think."

He listened for his instructions.

"Well, the bags we saw loaded into the semi could be farm supplies, fertilizers. It also could be something fairly easy to get but used for making bombs. And so we wondered what if that was not just a storage facility and that truck was not taking those supplies north of the border. What if it was delivering it to a bomb-making facility?"

Kyle listened as the rest of the team in the van stayed silent.

"Understood. I'll let them know."

"Guys, I think you are geniuses. They've just received word that there had been deliveries made to the compound in just small delivery vans for weeks. We thought it was food and supplies for the prisoners and the militia staying there, but apparently, they were also being delivered ammonium nitrate, and we know what they like to do with that, don't we? So I think we're on the money here. It's not drugs, and that would make sense based on Ochoa's proclivities, but it is indeed a staging or a bomb factory, and it's closer to the border than his compound, which would make his discoverability lessen. Nobody could accuse him of doing it at his place. I think it's a smart move, but we saw them."

Fredo said next what had to be said. "What we don't know is, do they know that we know?"

CHAPTER 16

MIA WOKE UP in an ambulance, screaming, while going like a bat out of Hell. She had a tube in her arm, and it appeared they were only giving her fluids. She checked her body to see if there was any pain, and other than a bruised lip and a small cut on her ear, she was fine. She had a bit of a headache, but otherwise, she was fine.

She opened her eyes and stared into the face of a paramedic.

"Ma'am, we're headed to the hospital, and we'll be there in just about five minutes. Do you have any medical conditions I need to know about?"

"Where am I?" She was confused and couldn't remember what happened. Then as she put her hand up to her forehead, she remembered that she had passed out and that she had apparently shot somebody.

"Did I kill someone?"

The two paramedics in the back chuckled. "Were

you going for that or were you just trying to scare him?" the other paramedic said.

"Stop fucking with me. Did I kill him or is he wounded?"

"Ma'am, he died in his own blood. He's being transported to the coroner. Apparently, there were lots of witnesses at the store. Was this man chasing you? Do you know who he was?"

"Absolutely no idea. But I think I know who sent him. I'll give you a complete statement. But first, I need you to call someone for me. I'm supposed to be over at Scripps by 1:00 to pick up a patient who's going to be living with us. I need to go do that."

"No can do, and it's already quarter to 1:00. You aren't going to make it."

"Then I need you to call over there or, better yet, do you have my purse?"

One of the medics handed her the bloodied purse. She looked at it incredulously. "Whose blood is this?"

"The guy you shot. He almost made it over to you. At least that's what the witnesses said, and he grabbed your purse and then was going for you."

"Okay, well, inside the purse—and you can go ahead and open it—there's a card of a Special Agent Gutierrez. I need you to call him and let him know what's happened. And then I need you to call the surgery ward at Scripps and let me talk to the head nurse there. I'm supposed to be picking up a patient, and I'm going to be late."

"Ma'am, they may admit you."

"That's horseshit. I'm not going to stay in any hospital. I've got to go get Ivan. And I'm going to bring him home no matter what you guys say. Nothing is going to keep me from doing that. Now if you're not going to take me to Scripps, because I'd agree to be seen at Scripps, then you better release me as soon as we get to the hospital. I'll say what I have to say so the doctor lets me go. But this is a life and death situation, and you have to let me do this."

"So where's your car?"

"At the grocery store where this guy fell. I left it there. The keys are probably still in it."

"No, the police probably took the keys, and they're probably going to impound the vehicle as well as the gentleman's vehicle."

"Crap. Something else I have to straighten out." She tried to calm herself and then added, "Would you please call and get permission to take me to Scripps? I got to get there right away."

After checking, they did receive permission to have her taken to the emergency room at Scripps, and they arrived at roughly ten minutes after 1:00. It was late, but she'd made it.

As they rolled her into the emergency room lobby,

she recognized several of the orderlies she had seen before on other occasions when she'd brought the children in for various things. They smiled and nodded, looking concerned, but finally, she recognized the smiling face of her neighbor, Anson Hernandez.

"Anson, Anson. It's Mia here."

The young attendant quickly made it to her side.

"Mia, what are you doing here? What happened?"

"There was an incident. Some man tried to kidnap me from the parking lot, and—"

"That was you?"

"Of course it was me. I told you it was me. Why?"

"The guy that was killed today a few minutes ago?"

"Yes, I guess. Unless there was another shooting."

She watched him tell her that it had been all over the news reports as an alert, and they'd sent alerts to all the area hospitals looking for anyone who knew anything about it, any eye witnesses.

"I am surprised that you were involved."

It was turning out to be that kind of a day.

"Why, you don't think I look like a serial killer? Well, it's not like I went after him. He came after me. He was going to take me in his car, and I found a pistol, and I shot him. That's all there is to it. But, Anson, I have another problem. I'm supposed to take a patient upstairs back to my house, and then I've got to go pick up the kids at school. I was supposed to bring them, but I was on my way to the store and never made it. So I've got my kids at the school waiting for me, and I've got the little boy I'm supposed to take home upstairs in the …"

"Mia, where's your cell phone? I can get the school's number out of your cell phone, right? And do you have someone else that could go pick the kids up?"

"I could try Christy or one of the other wives. There's Brandy and Libby Cooper."

"How about one of the soccer moms?"

"Good idea." She dialed the coach's wife, who promised she would have the kids delivered back home and would wait until she got there. "St. Cecilia, same as my Gordy goes to. I think I'm on file there and authorized to pick them up, right?"

"Yes. Oh, thank you!"

"Is everything okay Mia?" she asked.

"Well, now everything's fine, but we did have a near kidnapping incident. I'll explain it to you later. But please don't mention anything to the kids. Okay?"

The next call she made was to Christy.

"I saw that on the news. That was you?"

"Well, I didn't have much choice. It was his gun. I got it out of the glove box of the car. But, Christy, he tried to kidnap me. He tried to push me in the car and kidnap me. I'm here at Scripps, and I'm supposed to be taking Ivan back to my place."

"Oh, I didn't know that. I thought Kyle mentioned that he was going to go into some kind of a migrant camp for unaccompanied minors through CPS. I didn't realize you'd been given permission to take him."

"Gutierrez arranged it."

"Gutierrez? Did you know that Gutierrez has gone AWOL? Everybody's looking for him."

Oh, fuckin' crap-filled tamales. Why me?

"I'm missing something. I just talked to the man. In fact, he may be upstairs, here at the hospital. What do you mean?"

"Agent Gutierrez used to be an agent in high standing, but apparently, he works for the cartels now. Whatever he told you to do, Mia, he's probably directly put you in danger. I wouldn't trust him at all. The Feds are looking for him, and of course knowing that Fredo and Kyle had some interactions with him, half of SEAL Team 3 is looking for him too. He's moved out of his apartment. Apparently, he's just gone, disappeared."

"But I just talked to him…"

"On the phone, right? He could have been anywhere."

That told Mia everything she needed to know. They'd been completely duped. And she was all alone, hoping to rescue an orphan child, but she was the one that needed rescuing. And her children, now they were at risk as well. Her entire world was blowing up in front of her. And Fredo was on a mission, rescuing someone else's kids, probably.

It really wasn't fair.

She rolled off of the cart, almost falling on the floor, and stood on wobbly legs as Anson tried to help her. She was a mess. Her pants were torn, and her chest was covered in blood. Her hair was dusty and full of leaves.

"I've got to get upstairs to see Ivan. Anson, you've got to take me. And guys," she said as she turned to the paramedics, "I will settle up with you guys later. There's no way in hell I'm going to be admitted to this hospital. You tell the staff to just keep their distance. I'm a woman on a mission, and I will not be deterred! I will settle the bill as soon as I can, but right now, there's a little boy upstairs, and his life is in danger, and I've got to get there."

They reluctantly let Anson take her in the elevator to the fourth floor on the surgery wing. She passed by the charge nurse, who looked surprised to see her.

"I'm here to collect Ivan?"

"Ivan was checked out two hours ago, Mia. His representative came by signed all the paperwork. It had all been arranged in advance."

"You mean he's not here?"

"No, Mia. He's gone, checked out."

"Did he willingly go with this person?"

"I think so. Another of the nurses took care of him."

"This was a man, sort of a big man? With a short

mustache and dark black hair?"

"Yes, I think that was him. He signed it here. Right here, you see? It says Fred or Frederi-Fre—"

Mia read the name out loud. "Fredo Chavez. But that's my husband, and he's in Mexico."

"Well, they wouldn't have let him take the boy without a form of ID. How would they have that if your husband is in Mexico? Are you sure?"

"What? You think I would lie about something like that? I know I look a mess, but none of this is my fault. I'm being played here. Yes, I shot a man, but I was sent here to pick up this little migrant boy, and…"

Her tears burst out. She knew she looked crazy, and she did feel like a wreck.

"Would you like some juice?" the pretty candy striper asked.

"No! I'd like a pitcher of sangria!"

The young volunteer jumped back about two feet.

"I'm sorry. I know I don't make sense…"

Mia sat down on the leather bench, sobbing as she sunk into a deep despair. This was all wrong. She'd been outmaneuvered. They'd been too trusting, and the system had failed her. Now it was time to go around the system.

She called Julie Smith about meeting at her house, but the mother never answered her phone.

CHAPTER 17

FREDO AWOKE JUST before dawn when the valley floor was pink with the promise of a new day. At first, Fredo thought he would roll over on his bed but then realized they had not spent the night in the villa. They were still in the campout overlooking the villa and the compound beyond.

Hunching up on his elbows, he surveyed who was awake. People were beginning to stir, and close to the van, he saw Coop begin to get up and check his equipment. Fredo picked up his scope and aimed it down at their compound and didn't see anything unusual. There were no vehicles in the drive or along the roadway that led up to the villa. But as he scanned farther, Ochoa's compound was just beginning to come to life. He did notice one of the black Suburbans with its lights on, loading several people. He wished he had a better vantage point but whispered to get Coop's attention and pointed.

Coop had fashioned a special set of binoculars on his helmet, pulled them down, and took a look. He signaled that he identified something positive.

Fredo followed the roadway leading to the compound, and still everything was quiet. He listened for evidence of drone activity and wasn't able to hear a thing that bothered him.

He touched Kyle's bag and pointed toward the compound, handing him his scopes.

"Shit, something's going on. Okay, we got to go."

Kyle was up, and since they all were fully dressed, one by one, the team rousted themselves, patted Andy on the shoulder, thanking him for his night sentry, and began to mobilize. The best place for them to talk was inside one of the vans. It also was going to be the warmest place. The whole team gathered, huddled together, while Kyle waited for orders.

"Okay, so we got their attention. We're going to have to scope out whoever leaves this compound first. If it's one of the Suburbans, we follow it. If it's a civilian car, we follow it. I believe the theory is something has gone awry and Ochoa is leaving this morning. Coop, Fredo, anybody see what's happening with the cages down there?"

Coop responded first. "I see people spread out all over, sleeping, as best they can. But there does appear to be fewer people. Perhaps some have been taken away or loaded up somewhere. I'm pretty sure nothing happened last night, because I watched until the wee hours."

Fredo knew that Cooper had been tasked with getting all the rest he could since a highly trained medic was right now their most valuable asset if they were headed to a firefight. But he also knew that Coop had extra gadgets he'd brought, some of them not even Navy issue, and he just couldn't stay away from using all his "stuff," as he called it. He was also disciplined enough to operate with a lack of sleep for a few days, unlike anyone else Fredo had ever met.

He knew that all the tensions happening at home were beginning to weigh on him, and he was feeling his lack of sleep. Coop was the iron man, and he deserved it. He was the only one on the platoon today who didn't drink. Fredo thought perhaps he should give that a try as well. But damn, there were so many things coming down the road. And he stressed that he hadn't heard from Mia.

People began pouring out of the van, gathering their things, and they loaded up. Someone made some coffee that was poured around in tiny cups, which tasted delicious. A few energy bars were passed around, Kyle reminding them to stow the wrappers afterwards. That was going to be breakfast. Certainly wasn't like the breakfast he'd cooked for Mia a couple of days ago.

He smiled at that recollection.

"God, I hope you're safe," he said to himself and to her.

Kyle sauntered up to him and whispered in his ear. "Fredo, I guess Mia called Christy. You've got some voicemails you need to check. But I'm going to tell you not now. Okay?"

"Everyone okay?" He was rattled.

"I think so, just some news about something. And it was really short, and Christy should not have texted me. But I want you to know as soon as I know, so that's why I'm telling you."

"I got you. I've been staying off the phone. I only did one text yesterday."

"That's okay. There'll be time later, but right now, we got to focus here."

"Roger that."

So that was a hell of a thing. Now, Fredo had to worry about what he didn't know, and he didn't understand why he couldn't check his messages, but maybe there was something there that would affect his performance, and Kyle didn't want him to hear it. Whatever it was, he kind of wished that Kyle had kept his damn mouth shut. He took three deep breaths and went back to checking on the compound with his scopes.

The Suburban was being loaded with people, but it

didn't appear to be anyone from the prisoner cages. He wished to hell he had something higher power. He would've focused on all these images, but he was recording them, picking up his phone, and clicking the video on. Maybe if he sent it up to the LT, maybe they'd have a digital enhancement that could make out the faces of the movement he was watching.

"I'm going to send this up, Kyle. They're loading up one of the SUVs."

"Good." Kyle raised his own scopes and nodded. "Yep, I think it's going to be showtime very soon."

Then Kyle clicked his fingers, which got everyone's attention and pointed to his ear. Those who didn't have their Invisios inserted did so immediately, and he talked over the comms.

"So we got activity down there, and I want you to be packed up. If you don't have your bags in the van, get them in the van right now very quietly and very slowly. Remember, we're crab-like objects. Remember the beach training?"

A very soft groan arose from the group.

"I know, I know. But it got you to this day, and you're trained. And you're a badass."

Fredo heard a chuckle somewhere. They boarded the vans, and Fredo sat behind the wheel as he had before with Armando driving the other one. They turned over the engines and let them idle, warm up, and then waited.

Coop informed them that the Suburban was leaving the compound. The gates had been pulled back and allowed it to exit.

"That's our go-sign. Coop, can we send a drone or will that not be possible?"

"Not a good idea, sir. We're going to be traveling. I don't want to leave it behind. When we get to the road following the vehicle, I'll send it then if you want, but we'll have to stop. I got to make sure that she's locatable. If everybody's moving, it's going to be problematic. And if that drone drops and they see it, well, they're going to know everything. They're going to even get the camera that's on it. So we can't do that."

"I got that. All right, let's move out. Slowly."

They wound down through the back road, avoiding the turnoff for the compound they had been staying at earlier. Pausing at the junction of the official road and the driveway, however, even though both of them were gravel, Fredo checked right and left and then without seeing traffic turned left as he was instructed. Kyle was talking to his LT, and they had visual contact of the vehicle, which was helpful.

This time, the SUV headed due west, appearing to head to the village, not north to the area where they found the semi at the edge of the mountain. There was a detour that came up on Kyle's computer sent by San

Diego, indicating the Suburban had turned and was going to circumvent the village, not go through the middle. He continued getting instructions from home, which he relayed to Fredo. They sped up slightly so they could close the gap, and Fredo finally saw the taillights of the Suburban way off in the distance. Due to the fact the terrain was so completely flat, except for small clumps of trees and swales, creek beds in wintertime, their visibility was as at least fifty miles in any one direction.

Kyle's instructions alerted a change in course, the Suburban heading due north.

"I think they're heading for the border, Gents. Looks like we might get our opportunity here."

Fredo was excited with the news. At last, perhaps something was going to be actually happening. He knew the waiting was always necessary, especially being able to understand their environment and where all the players were located. Waiting and studying was always a good idea, and when things happened spur of the moment, it often led to unintended consequences and a possible firefight, which was dangerous. But this team had twelve able-bodied men, and he guessed that there weren't twelve shooters in that suburban. Probably only a handful, if Ochoa was one of them.

They followed the van at a distance, but Fredo kept his line of sight since the light of the morning made it possible for him to turn off his headlights. The Suburban was traveling approximately eighty-five miles an hour, so Fredo had to floor the van to keep up.

Kyle got word that the vehicle was indeed heading for a border crossing, something not official, but an area where there was free passage if someone had a four-wheel drive vehicle and could traverse a small rivulet coming off the Rio Grande. He knew that oftentimes the cartels used dried up creek beds as highways, which would cover up their tire tracks after occasional rains here, and make numerous trips almost undetectable.

Kyle was alerted that they had a go for stopping the vehicle. "Can you catch up to him, Fredo?" Kyle asked.

"I'm flooring it now, but I'll give it some more if I can. These things don't have the power the Suburban does, but I'm trying."

The SUV began to slow and then pulled to the side of the road and drove down into a creek bed valley. This was a lucky break for the SEALs, because that meant the trip would be slower and it was now possible for Fredo to overtake them, if he could close the gap. They were following behind in clouds of dust, gravel, and rocks that had been spewed all over the area. It wasn't lost on Fredo that it was possible the targets didn't even know he was following them, there was such a dust storm created from its massive tires.

"We have orders to ram him. Let's go." Kyle said over the comms.

Fredo stepped on it, and within seconds, the caked back end of the Suburban and its red taillights flashed. Fredo drove right into him and knocked the suburban in the driver's side rear panel, knocking it at an angle and causing an overcorrection from the driver, which nearly toppled the vehicle, but it was still moving, and Fredo now was concerned about the condition of the front end of his van.

"How's everybody back there?"

"Good to go. Van B is right behind us. Thank God they didn't hit us, because I'm sure they can't see a damn thing."

"Okay, do it again. We have instructions to stop and board."

Fredo hit the SUV one more time, and this time bent the left rear tire, causing the Suburban to swerve back and forth, fishtailing, and finally resting, slammed up next to the side of the rivulet bank. Within seconds, the doors opened, and they were being fired on with automatic weapons. Van B flew past them and crossed the path where the shooters were taking some of the firepower, but enabling Fredo's van to unload. Everyone spread out and took positions so that when the dust settled, they were ready to mark and hit anybody they could see.

At this distance, Fredo didn't need his scopes, but he grabbed his MP3 and was wearing extra clips, rolled out of the van, but left the motor running. He followed Coop behind a couple of scrubs, surveyed the perimeter, and noted there were fewer shots coming from the area of the SUV. He also noticed two bodies next to the driver's side door, the door hanging open but riddled with bullets. Fredo knew Ochoa had to be there, and he also knew they were required to bring him in alive.

Kyle reminded everyone for a sighting. "Anybody, anybody see those green boots, you let me know. Everybody else here is expendable."

"Roger that," said Fredo. He took up a position quickly behind a small tree, which didn't give him much stopping power or protection but gave him a better vantage point. Then he saw movement on the opposite side of the Suburban. Grabbing his binoculars, he honed it at dirt level and saw the unmistakable green boots running in the opposite direction away from the vehicle.

"I got eyes on him," Fredo said, just as two others communicated the same thing.

They took off after Ochoa. Kyle and six others stayed behind and immobilized, pinning down the remaining shooters until at last there were no more shots fired. The desert was eerily quiet as they ran full tilt up a small swale where Ochoa had scrambled and dove over the edge. They didn't know what was going to be there, but they had to follow.

Fredo took point, and the three others spread out maneuvering so that, when given the call, they could take the ridge. When Fredo got up to the top, he saw Ochoa scaling down a rocky riverbed wall, heading for a small stream, but he was all alone. He gave the order for the group to advance, and the SEALs were able to overtake Ochoa, mostly because of those damn green boots that were probably too small for him.

Vanity proved to be his undoing. Fredo grabbed the guy, faced him straight on nose to nose, while his team tied Ochoa up.

"Okay, motherfucker, you get a free trip to visit your Uncle Sam. Have a nice day." He said and ran to the side to report to Kyle that they had captured him.

Fredo noticed that his van was smoking when he reached the ridge line and surveyed the group. All of the shooters from the Suburban had been either incapacitated, wounded, or killed. The vehicle was not drivable. They were ordered to leave the dead and wounded in place. Kyle ordered the whole team to pile into the second van, get nice and cozy with Ochoa, and head for the point of entry at the border. Fredo was tasked to drive.

It had been arranged that a US representative would meet them after they got through Mexican authorities, but they would not have help until they got through the Mexican side. They were instructed not to show papers or passports, and if necessary to blow past the gates. The Mexican authorities were not going to be notified of their crossing, but once San Diego learned that they had blown through, they would do so immediately to stop any further action, if possible. But they were prepared for another firefight. Ochoa was covered up, and as they approached the gate, he began to yell in Spanish, swearing like a stuffed pig. Coop took out a tourniquet and a rag from his medic kit and subdued his mouth. He pulled the tarp back over the gentleman, and then everybody waited as Fredo slowed and eventually stopped at the checkpoint.

"Your papers please, passports, and destination," the border guard asked in Spanish.

Fredo told him that they had been messed with by Ochoa and his militia and that they were coming. He had to move his men through the border, and if Ochoa came, he should let them pass and not try to stop them. He explained to them that these were construction workers, all US citizens, and this was a rescue mission to free them from being captive.

The border guard looked through the windows and noticed the overcrowding situation. He didn't do much checking, so Fredo knew that his little story about Ochoa and his militia had created a good ruse. The border guard didn't want to have anything to do with Mr. Ochoa. Fredo suspected that he would take a vantage point and abandon his post until the militia or what he thought was going to be the militia came through.

Fredo traveled the stretch between the two borders. Kyle got word that the SOS had gone out to the Mexican authorities about a rescue operation and requesting they have permission to leave the country, which was unnecessary but part of the plan.

At the US side, they all breathed the sigh of relief. They were waved through, and Kyle had a visual map of an airstrip they were to wait for a pickup.

Approximately forty-five minutes later, they arrived at the airport or what could be called a farmer's landing strip, really. They were peppered all over the border area for light planes and even larger planes to take off and land from. It was almost like the whole region was perfect for an airport without ever having to build one.

Ochoa was given a tranquilizing shot and would be coming on board as a wounded passenger, but fully restrained by his wrists and ankles. He hadn't been wounded, that is, not his body. But he was furious. His red face and bloodshot eyes spewed hatred, and his language was vile, so Coop gave him another dose, and he immediately dozed off. Fredo and Armando laughed at some of his expressions, and they were grateful the rest of the group didn't understand them.

Finally, the small jet landed, not exactly a fine-looking specimen, but this bucket of bolts was going to be their lifesaver. The pilot taxied then turned around and headed back in the direction in which he came, ready for takeoff. They abandoned the van, loaded all the equipment, and three people took Ochoa on a makeshift stretcher. Everybody loaded up, and in less than five minutes, they were wheels up and headed to San Diego.

Kyle informed them that it was a straight shot, no stops, and they'd be home soon.

A cheer went up. Mission accomplished.

The one thing that Fredo needed next was to hear from Mia. He hoped to God she had some good news for him.

CHAPTER 18

G US MAYFIELD ARRIVED at the police station where Mia was being interviewed. A task force had been created from there to find Ivan and former Agent Gutierrez, as well as Mia's soccer mom friend, Julie Smith, her three children, and Mia and Fredo's three.

Mayfield slowly and delicately told Mia he'd been informed that three armed guards had shown up at the school just as her friend was leaving with the kids and diverted her and the children. It happened so fast there wasn't time for administrators to intervene. Someone had tried to follow them and got shot at on the highway so turned off and reported the incident to police. Numerous other parents and teachers also called in the event.

"Oh my God, oh please, please, please, please, please, they have to be safe!"

Mayfield held Mia in his massive arms, trying to reassure her, but she was inconsolable.

"And Ivan. Ivan is missing too."

"Well, I think they have ways of tracking Gutierrez, so I give that a pretty good chance of finding them."

What Mayfield didn't say and Mia feared was if the child proved to be too much baggage for Gutierrez, that he might damage him or worse.

"So he's headed for the border?" she asked.

"We believe so. But you stay here while I check around and see what I can find out. Have you heard from Fredo?"

"Well, he said if he didn't call me back, I wasn't to call him. They sometimes go places that they're not allowed to use the cell."

"Fuck that. You get him on the phone. This is important," Mayfield shouted.

Mia quickly dialed Fredo's number. Astonishingly enough, he picked up on the first ring.

"*Mi amore!*"

"Sweetheart, I just listened to your messages. I'm so sorry I wasn't able to respond. Are you okay? Are the kids okay? And how is Ivan?"

Mia didn't know where to start. Her emotions were beginning to take over again, and she stammered and sputtered. In between tears and moments of clarity, she tried to communicate all the facts as she knew them. "And all of this could be different now. It turns out, Fredo, nothing we were told was the truth. Agent

SHARON HAMILTON

Gutierrez works for the cartels!"

"Fuck it. That asshole. I just hope he gets justice, we get justice."

"No, Fredo. You don't do anything, okay? We have to focus on getting the kids back. We just want to find the kids."

"I'm going to see if I can get released. We dropped off Ochoa, and we're headed back to base. I'll get there as fast as I can."

She had given him the station name and address and looked for Mayfield so she could let him know that Fredo was on his way.

It was a long forty-five minutes. The police station was a beehive of activity, and Mia sat in the corner, wrapped in a metal blanket, because she was shivering. Finally, someone came over and felt her forehead, took her pulse, and determined she needed to lie down and rest until her husband arrived. All the questions she had for them went unanswered. They had to nicely tell her to stop interfering and let them do their job.

Mayfield escorted her into an empty office/storage room that had a cot and several fresh pillows and blankets.

"You lay down here and cover up, and I'm going to be right outside this door. I'm not going to leave. I'm going to stay right here until you wake up, okay?"

Mia was in a strange state. She needed the rest. But

she felt oddly strong, mentally. Adrenaline was pumping through her big time, yet her body was still failing her. She sat on the cot and removed her shoes while Gus positioned the pillow for her head and covered her with a blanket.

Lying down had never felt so good.

Mayfield dipped down to whisper in her ear, "Mia, sweetheart, you just relax and let it all go. You're going to be safe, everything's going to work out, you'll see. Just wait here for Fredo. You're doing great, kid. You're doing really great."

As Mia fell into a deep sleep, she somehow could tell that her stepfather wanted to give her a kiss on the cheek, but he was awkward and unsure of himself, which was the reason her mother loved him so much.

"Thank you, Gus." And then she fell asleep.

FREDO'S WARM ARMS pulling her into his chest and squeezing her tight awakened every single pore in her body. She smelled his sweat, his unique scent, the sounds he made as he mumbled in her ear and pressed her close.

"You're safe. You're safe, and there are lots of people looking for the kids. Oh, Mia, thank God you're okay. What you have been through and what I have let you—"

Mia put her fingers over his mouth. "Kiss me, Fredo."

They kissed gently, and then her need for his reassurance overcame her, and she pressed closer to him. "Hold me."

"Of course, Sweetheart, I'm here. We will not leave any stone unturned."

"I don't know why I'm so tired. I'm exhausted from all of this. And we had such high hopes for Ivan and our plans for the future, and I just don't know what's going to happen."

"Well, we first have to find everybody. So you've got to help us. Is there anything you can tell us about the plans about where you think Gutierrez would go? Anything?"

She racked her brain trying to think of something that could help them. But nothing was coming. "I'm just blank. It's like I can hardly remember anything that's happened. It's all a blur. I have so much racing around my head…"

His palm brushed back the hair from her forehead. "You're just exhausted, and now it's time for others to do the heavy lifting. Your part is done for now. I know it's difficult, but we're going to have to wait until they finish, and they will find them, I know they will."

"I think of Ivan too, how terrified he must be. You think they'll coordinate somehow? They put everybody together somewhere? That's the only thing I can think of, Fredo. These two parts have to be working together, right?"

"I think that's what they're working on. Gus is out there trying to be a fly on the wall. He's kind of big, and he sort of sticks out, so we'll see how well that goes. But for now, at least, they haven't kicked him out. Gus said these guys here are really good. And he's worked with them for years. I think it's good that he's here."

"So how did your mission go?"

"Mission accomplished. Ochoa was delivered, hand delivered you might say. Boy, he was angry. It'll be interesting to see what impact that has. We still have to negotiate with the Mexican authorities, since he was a fugitive from them technically and a former federal officer. But I'm sure our guys aren't going to let him go home anytime soon, and he's probably going to spend quite a few years behind bars here. It sucks though. It'll be a lot more luxurious than it would be in any kind of prison in Mexico. Trust me on that."

"Sounds like he doesn't even deserve that. But I'm glad you got him. Any word on the caravan people who perished?"

"Well, that's gonna depend on him, and we did get some positive news on the photos that I sent out. It looks like that's verification that Ochoa had been involved with this group, so that adds an extra layer of depth to his future prison sentence. I'll just put it that way, because in all reality, it's going to take years before he'll be convicted. But he's going to remain behind bars where he can't hurt anybody else. But they'll find somebody else to run the operation. They always do."

"I'm so glad you were able to do that. Ivan is going to be thrilled with this. I can't wait for you to tell him."

Fredo paused for a few seconds and then delicately approached his next idea.

"You know, we have to prepare for the possibility that they may do away with Ivan, as he's not the package or the prize for them if they sell him, but he's also the problem. He's the only one who can link that group with Ochoa, on an eyewitness basis because he was there. We have the photos, but he can tell the Feds a whole lot more about the operation. In that sense, him being alive is dangerous. So I don't want you to expect it, but I want you to be prepared in case we get some bad news. That's how these things go. I've seen it myself many times overseas."

Mia's tears soaked her cheeks and the top of her blouse. But she was controlled. "I understand. We tried, we really tried, Fredo. I did it because I wanted to give him a better life. I will forever feel partially responsible for this."

Fredo tried to silence her, but she wouldn't be

hushed. "No. Let me continue. I trusted the wrong people, and because of my actions and my need to fulfill that promise to myself, I acted without thinking. I was stupid, Fredo."

"No, Sweetheart. You were brave. You did what any caring mother would do, and more. I mean, you defended yourself against an armed assailant. No one lost their lives over it in that grocery store except for the bad guy. You got word to the right people, and now it's up to them to do what they do best. Ivan was never going to be a happy youngster in a wonderful, loving home. He was trafficked, Mia. Everything he had in life had been ripped from him. He was a pawn, being used still by the people who originally were responsible for his leaving his home to come to the States. His mother made that decision, bringing him all this way and exposing all of them to such danger. And look at what they aspired to, to find a man who may not know that Ivan exists and may not even want him? I mean, if you look at his odds, Mia, they weren't good to begin with, sweetheart. But don't blame yourself. It's why this whole trafficking business is so tragic. It's not only tragic for the person who's being abused, but everybody who tries to help them. Everybody surrounding that person, their family at home, other people, innocent people, get caught in that web. It's the nature of the business. It's brutal, it's bloody, and they absolutely don't care about you or me or our children or Ivan, for that matter. It's the reality of the situation, Mia."

She was grateful for Fredo's honesty and for the reminder that she still was a mother of three boys and that was her job, her only job.

The door burst open, and Mayfield's hulking frame blocked the entire doorway. "We got a hit. We know where Gutierrez's car is. They're going to see if perhaps he's met up with the others, but they're going to get him. It's just a matter of time."

Mia noticed his face was the most hopeful she'd seen. "Thank you."

"So I'm going to go check things out here and get a full read on everything. Mia, you stay here, okay?" whispered Fredo.

"Not on your life. I'm going to go everywhere you go. You're not leaving me behind this time."

Fredo smiled at her. "Of course, Dear." And then he smiled again.

Mia was reminded of the counseling session they had gone to at one time when they hit a rocky patch in their marriage. And the counselor had clearly told Fredo that the best thing he could do when his wife was upset about something was to first answer back, "Yes, dear."

"You remembered."

"Absolutely. I remembered all of it. I remember all

the good and only this much," he held his thumb and first finger together to show how small, "this much of the bad stuff."

Within minutes, Gutierrez's car was located, parked at a motel about twenty miles from the border station near San Diego. It was frequented by relatives coming to greet other relatives coming across the border. It was explained to Mia and Fredo that when Gutierrez became a suspect, when they called in the FBI to surveil him and possibly do an assessment of whether or not he was compromised, they put a tracking device on several of the things he would be taking. One of them was his suitcase, which he had with him always, but the other tracking device, in addition to things planted at his home, was on the car. And Gutierrez had not switched the car out. Hence, they knew where he had been and hopefully was now.

As Fredo and Mia watched, they received news that a SWAT team had arrived, verified with the clerk at the front desk that, in fact, Gutierrez was there, and he also verified that he was with a young boy. The clerk said it bothered him to see how frail and scared the young boy looked. He suspected that he was either a runaway or had paid this gentleman or someone else to bring him over the border, and now was beholden to him.

They weren't able to see the videos, but the SWAT team did wear body cameras, and the police verified that, in fact, Gutierrez was in the room with Ivan. They were both very much alive. While they were processing the scene and separating Ivan from Gutierrez, his accomplice arrived with Mrs. Smith and the children, all six of them. Everybody was fine. The police stopped the vehicle in the parking lot, unloaded everybody, and arrested the three gunmen. They found directions, pictures, maps, and a ton of arms and ammunition. They also found some drugs. The kids were fine and anxious to come home.

"Even after all that's happened, Fredo, I still want to fight for Ivan. Now, I want to give him that American future more than ever. Can we do this?"

"As long as you don't get your hopes up. It might be difficult, but I agree. It's going to be tight, Mia. But I'm all for it, Sweetheart. He deserves you as his mother."

CHAPTER 19

FREDO WAS GRATEFUL beyond words as the big police van pulled up with his precious cargo, bounding down the stairs, high-fiving police and rescuers. Ricardo was right in the middle of it all, and the Smith kids couldn't stop talking about riding in the big tactical van and meeting all the officers who helped in their rescue. He imagined it was like living inside their favorite police movie. They had probably not really realized or considered how much danger they were in. He knew that, for weeks to come, they'd be the talk of the school. The director might even hold an assembly to talk about child safety and human trafficking—but all that was someone else's job.

The only thing that worried him was little Ivan, who had been pitched from one country to another, losing those he loved and getting let down by those he had quickly formed an attachment to who he probably felt had let him down. Again.

He kept to the sides and watched as their three children ran to their mother, and she embraced them with a big wide happy smile on her face, tears and all. It was quite a reunion, and Fredo would never forget this day.

He sauntered over to Ivan, stood next to him, and watched just like he did. He sensed if he tried to put an arm around the kid, he'd pull away. It was going to take a lot of time, and Fredo knew he could be patient. He'd seen so much about this kid already that he knew he'd survive all this. And if they let him, Fredo and Mia could turn his wishes into dreams.

He wished he could help every single suffering child everywhere. But of course, those lofty goals could never be fully achieved. And it probably would take some of these kids growing up and healing, if they could, to help such a project get off the ground.

But that was a wish and a dream for another day. Right now, Ivan had support around him that he wouldn't allow himself to accept. His fixation was on Mia and the kids, Julie Smith's kids jumping up and down, excited like they'd just been on a carnival ride. Nobody was paying attention to Ivan, but he saw it all, and he compared his life to theirs.

Fredo knew it was making him sadder by the minute. He was lost again.

He knelt down in front of the boy. He did not

touch him. The scared look on Ivan's face told Fredo he'd been right.

"Ivan, I'm so proud of you," he said in Spanish. "This has been no picnic. You've been living with this uncertainty for weeks now, if not years. But I'm here to tell you that's going to be all over soon. Just like we promised, we're going to make sure you have a loving home, our home, if we're allowed. We'd like to include you in our family. I think there's a lot you could teach our kids about what life is elsewhere. They don't know anything but this. You know so much more."

His little mouth was still pursed shut, almost in defiance against his own emotions. Fredo knew Ivan wanted to be needed like his kids. Being left out was one of the first things he probably learned in his young years. He probably had no real childhood. Everything had been robbed from him and nobody really cared.

"Would you like me to help you find your father, the Marine?"

His attention immediately went back to Fredo's face, although he suppressed the glimmer of hope Fredo saw behind Ivan's eyes.

"No promises, but we'll do our best to locate him. If it doesn't work out, I hope that you'll consider living with us, allowing us to become your parents, legally. Unless you'd rather go back to Mexico to live with your siblings?"

He shook his head. His first words were, "I don't like that place anymore."

"Okay, then should we look for your father?"

He nodded his head, yes.

That hurt more than Fredo had expected it to. He would have much preferred Ivan to choose him over an absent father, albeit, a father who didn't know he existed. But that was Ivan's choice, and not one Fredo could make for him.

He was giving Ivan a taste of the freedom he so desperately wanted and didn't know how to ask for.

"You know, when I saw you standing there, facing that gun pointed at you, you stood tall. You are very, very brave, Ivan. Never forget that. I know what bravery is all about, and I've seen good and bad examples of it. That's part of what haunts me every day. But I believe, if we stay strong and we work together as a team, we can accomplish anything. Do you believe that, Ivan?"

The kid swallowed hard, and then Fredo saw the tears forming. Slowly, Ivan moved towards him and then fell against his chest and began to sob.

In that heartbreakingly wonderful moment, he knew what his real mission in life was. He was a protector, yes. A defender of his country. And he was husband to the most wonderful woman in the world.

But most of all, he was a father. He had been destined for that even when he thought he couldn't father a child of his own and beat those odds, with the help of Coop and his ridiculous smoothies and tofu. He won Mia's heart in the beginning, which started his journey. He'd been witness to some of the finest men ever created. He'd put away some real assholes. And he still came back, because he was father to these boys. And, even if Ivan didn't choose to live with them, Fredo would always feel like a father to the boy and would always be there for him, no matter what.

Ivan's little sobs died down as Fredo's palm rubbed his back and squeezed the top of his spine, speaking to him in his native tongue.

There would be time for speeches later, lessons on living, and reflections. Right now, he was just grateful today would end on a bright note. He hoped he'd lit a candle for Ivan so he could see his way forward when it got dark again.

And he hoped it never got dark.

ALL FOUR OF the boys were splashing in the pool. Ivan stayed in the shallow end, on the sand deck, and Fredo suspected he'd never been in a real pool before and probably didn't know how to swim. But he wasn't going to embarrass him by placing water wings on his arms or a life preserver. Fredo would watch vigilantly and protect him from that humiliation.

He thought perhaps Ricardo and the twins might have figured all that out, and they played gently in the sand deck area, not the deep end like they usually did. It made no difference as the same amount of water was splashed, just without all the jumping in and out.

Ricardo offered to share his room with Ivan, and that upset the twins. Fredo watched Ivan's face as he laughed at being the most popular one, for a change. In the end, he chose to room with Ricardo.

They didn't know in the days that followed if Ricardo ever told Ivan about his biological dad, or "sperm donor," but on the day when Caesar had made the appointment to come see Ricardo, everyone in the household was on edge with this highly anticipated meeting.

Mia especially was unsure whether or not they were doing the right thing. She'd discussed how she still feared repercussions from the cartel bosses or others who associated with the former agent, Gutierrez.

"You worry too much, Mia. Look at what we've been through. You think God would have put all of us through this if he didn't have a plan? We're not done yet."

"Whatever do you mean?"

"I don't know. I guess this has made me realize there is more to life than what I do. My family has always been important to me. But I look at little Ivan, and I'm inspired."

"What are you going to do if he finds his father and goes away?"

"Ask him about his mother. He'll tell you. He's very smart. It will be like the answer he gave me when I asked him if he missed her. He put his palm right here, on his heart," Fredo placed Mia's hand on his heart, "And said to me, 'she is right here.'"

They waited for an hour for Caesar to show up. He was supposed to arrive at two. Half past three, it finally dawned on them all, especially Ricardo, that his father wasn't coming. With no phone call, no message left, they didn't know what happened. Ricardo was in a slump for the next two days because of it. Fredo witnessed how Ivan was tender with him. Did little things to make him laugh. Ricardo could be glum around Mia and Fredo, but Ivan's personality was infectious, and he could not resist breaking a smile when the little one did his antics to cheer him up. They became closer than Fredo thought possible, each boy healing the other one's heart.

Mayfield one day revealed that Caesar had been arrested again for dealing drugs and pimping and was likely to spend another few years in prison.

"You suppose he ever intended to meet Ricardo?" Fredo asked.

"We don't know, do we? No father should put his

kid through that. Something's wrong with a man who can't be a man."

"Roger that."

About a month later, as they were sitting around the dining table, the subject of fatherhood came up. One of the twins had used "sperm donor" in a derogatory way in his conversation, and Mia stopped him. Ricardo was shaken but tried not to show it.

Fredo called to him, and Ricardo sat next to him on the table's bench seat.

"I'm going to tell you something about fatherhood, real fatherhood." He spoke to the whole group assembled there. "Anyone, well, almost anyone can father a child. But a real father is part of his son's life. And he does things in life to make sure he gets to stay that way. Ricardo's biological father, I believe, really wanted to be a good father. Who wouldn't?"

He messed up the top of Ricardo's hair, and the rest of the boys laughed.

"But it takes someone who makes better choices to be a real father. And when you guys grow up, I hope you'll remember that. Fathers don't just happen. They're a complicated mixture of bailing wire, bravery, honor, duty, and…"

He looked across the table at Mia.

"And love." He smiled at her.

He heard her whisper "*Mi Amore*."

Ricardo put his arm around Fredo and gave him a hug. And then he heard the words he could not believe.

"I'm glad you're my real dad."

Ivan held his orange juice up for a toast. He stood on their side of the bench.

"To real dads everywhere, whether they know it or not!"

His English wasn't perfect, but it went straight to everyone's heart as they all toasted to the best of the days to come.

ABOUT THE AUTHOR

 NYT and USA/Today Bestselling Author Sharon Hamilton's SEAL Brotherhood series have earned her author rankings of #1 in Romantic Suspense, Military Romance and Contemporary Romance. Her other *Brotherhood* stand-alone series are: Bad Boys of SEAL Team 3, Band of Bachelors, True Blue SEALs, Nashville SEALs, Bone Frog Brotherhood, Sunset SEALs, Bone Frog Bachelor Series and SEAL Brotherhood Legacy Series. She is a contributing author to the very popular Shadow SEALs multi-author series.

Her SEALs and former SEALs have invested in two wineries, a lavender farm and a brewery in Sonoma County, which have become part of the new stories. They also have expanded to include Veteran-benefit projects on the Florida Gulf Coast, as well as projects in Africa and the Maldives. One of the SEAL wives has even launched her own women's fiction series. But old characters, as well as children of these SEAL heroes keep returning to all the newer books.

Sharon also writes sexy paranormals in two series: Golden Vampires of Tuscany and The Guardians under the pen name S. Hamil. She has a new Sci-Fi series, Free to Love, coming out in June of 2023 in a five book ultra-spicy series about an Android who falls in love with a human woman.

Annie Carr, Sharon's sweet romance author pen name, has just released her first book in 2023, I'll Always Love You, in Sunset Beach stories. She is planning this to become a multiple-book series.

A lifelong organic vegetable and flower gardener, Sharon and her husband lived for fifty years in the Wine Country of Northern California, where many of her stories take place. Recently, they have moved to the beautiful Gulf Coast of Florida, with stories of ship-wrecks, the white sugar-sand beaches of Sunset, Treasure Island and Indian Rocks Beaches.

She loves hearing from fans through her website:
authorsharonhamilton.com

Find out more about Sharon, her upcoming releases, appearances and news when you sign up for Sharon's newsletter.

Facebook:
facebook.com/SharonHamiltonAuthor

Twitter:
twitter.com/sharonlhamilton

Pinterest:
pinterest.com/AuthorSharonH

Amazon:
amazon.com/Sharon-Hamilton/e/B004FQQMAC

BookBub:
bookbub.com/authors/sharon-hamilton

Youtube:
youtube.com/channel/UCDInkxXFpXp_4Vnq08ZxMBQ

Soundcloud:
soundcloud.com/sharon-hamilton-1

Sharon Hamilton's Rockin' Romance Readers:
facebook.com/groups/sealteamromance

Sharon Hamilton's Goodreads Group:
goodreads.com/group/show/199125-sharon-hamilton-readers-group

Visit Sharon's Online Store:
sharon-hamilton-author.myshopify.com

Join Sharon's Review Teams:

eBook Reviews:
sharonhamiltonassistant@gmail.com

Audio Reviews:
sharonhamiltonassistant@gmail.com

Life is one fool thing after another.
Love is two fool things after each other.

REVIEWS

PRAISE FOR THE
GOLDEN VAMPIRES OF TUSCANY SERIES

"Well to say the least I was thoroughly surprise. I have read many Vampire books, from Ann Rice to Kym Grosso and few other Authors, so yes I do like Vampires, not the super scary ones from the old days, but the new ones are far more interesting far more human than one can remember. I found Honeymoon Bite a totally engrossing book, I was not able to put it down, page after page I found delight, love, understanding, well that is until the bad bad Vamp started being really bad. But seeing someone love another person so much that they would do anything to protect them, well that had me going, then well there was more and for a while I thought it was the end of a beautiful love story that spanned not only time but, spanned Italy and California. Won't divulge how it ended, but I did shed a few tears after screaming but Sharon Hamilton did not let me down, she took me on amazing trip that I loved, look forward to reading another Vampire book of hers."

"An excellent paranormal romance that was exciting, romantic, entertaining and very satisfying to read. It had me anticipating what would happen next many times over, so much so I could not put it down and even finished it up in a day. The vampires in this book were different from your average vampire, but I enjoy different variations and changes to the same old stuff. It made for a more unpredictable read and more adventurous to explore! Vampire lovers, any paranormal readers and even those who love the romance genre will enjoy Honeymoon Bite."

"This is the first non-Seal book of this author's I have read and I loved it. There is a cast-like hierarchy in this vampire community with humans at the very bottom and Golden vampires at the top. Lionel is a dark vampire who are servants of the Goldens. Phoebe is a Golden who has not decided if she will remain human or accept the turning to become a vampire. Either way she and Lionel can never be together since it is forbidden.

I enjoyed this story and I am looking forward to the next installment."

"A hauntingly romantic read. Old love lost and new love found. Family, heart, intrigue and vampires. Grabbed my attention and couldn't put down. Would definitely recommend."

PRAISE FOR THE
SEAL BROTHERHOOD SERIES

"Fans of Navy SEAL romance, I found a new author to feed your addiction. Finely written and loaded delicious with moments, Sharon Hamilton's storytelling satisfies like a thick bar of chocolate." —Marliss Melton, bestselling author of the *Team Twelve* Navy SEALs series

"Sharon Hamilton does an EXCELLENT job of fitting all the characters into a brotherhood of SEALS that may not be real but sure makes you feel that you have entered the circle and security of their world. The stories intertwine with each book before...and each book after and THAT is what makes Sharon Hamilton's SEAL Brotherhood Series so very interesting. You won't want to put down ANY of her books and they will keep you reading into the night when you should be sleeping. Start with this book...and you will not want to stop until you've read the whole series and then...you will be waiting for Sharon to write the next one." (5 Star Review)

"Kyle and Christy explode all over the pages in this first book, *[Accidental SEAL]*, in a whole new series of SEALs. If the twist and turns don't get your heart jumping, then maybe the suspense will. This is a must read for those that are looking for love and adventure with a little sloppy love thrown in for good measure." (5 Star Review)

PRAISE FOR THE
BAD BOYS OF SEAL TEAM 3 SERIES

"I love reading this series! Once you start these books, you can hardly put them down. The mix of romance and suspense keeps you turning the pages one right after another! Can't wait until the next book!" (5 Star Review)

"I love all of Sharon's Seal books, but *[SEAL's Code]* may just be her best to date. Danny and Luci's journey is filled with a wonderful insight into the Native American life. It is a love story that will fill you with warmth and contentment. You will enjoy Danny's journey to become a SEAL and his reasons for it. Good job Sharon!" (5 Star Review)

PRAISE FOR THE
BAND OF BACHELORS SERIES

"*[Lucas]* was the first book in the Band of Bachelors series and it was a phenomenal start. I loved how we got to see the other SEALs we all love and we got a look at Lucas and Marcy. They had an instant attraction, and their love was very intense. This book had it all, suspense, steamy romance, humor, everything you want in a riveting, outstanding read. I can't wait to read the next book in this series." (5 Star Review)

PRAISE FOR THE
TRUE BLUE SEALS SERIES

"Keep the tissues box nearby as you read *True Blue SEALs: Zak* by Sharon Hamilton. I imagine more than I wish to that the circumstances surrounding Zak and Amy are all too real for returning military personnel and their families. Ms. Hamilton has put us right in the middle of struggles and successes that these two high school sweethearts endure. I have read several of Sharon Hamilton's military romances but will say this is the most emotionally intense of the ones that I have read. This is a well-written, realistic story with authentic characters that will have you rooting for them and proud of those who serve to keep us safe. This is an author who writes amazing stories that you love and cry with the characters. Fans of Jessica Scott and Marliss Melton will want to add Sharon Hamilton to their list of realistic military romance writers." (5 Star Review)

"Dear FATHER IN HEAVEN,

If I may respectfully say so sometimes you are a strange God. Though you love all mankind,

It seems you have special predilections too.

You seem to love those men who can stand up alone who face impossible odds, Who challenge every bully and every tyrant ~

Those men who know the heat and loneliness of Calvary. Possibly you cherish men of this stamp because you recognize the mark of your only son in them.

Since this unique group of men known as the SEALs know Calvary and suffering, teach them now the mystery of the resurrection ~ that they are indestructible, that they will live forever because of their deep faith in you.

And when they do come to heaven, may I respectfully warn you, Dear Father, they also know how to celebrate. So please be ready for them when they insert under your pearly gates.

Bless them, their devoted Families and their Country on this glorious occasion.

We ask this through the merits of your Son, Christ Jesus the Lord, Amen."

By Reverend E.J. McMalhon S.J. LCDR, CHC, USN
Awards Ceremony SEAL Team One
1975 At NAB, Coronado

www.ingramcontent.com/pod-product-compliance
Lightning Source LLC
Chambersburg PA
CBHW051945220626
47052CB00004B/804